I0598612

A Wave of Thanks

And Other Human Gestures

31 Quick Stories

Other Books
by Bear Jack Gebhardt
(See them all on Amazon.com)

- *The Smoker's Prayer: Spiritual Healing of Tobacco Addiction*

- *Happy John: An Advaita (Non-Duality) Gospel*

- *Practicing the Presence of Peace*

- *The Potless Pot High: How to Get High, Clear and Spunky without Weed*

- *How to Stop Smoking in 15 Easy Years: A Slacker's Guide to Final Freedom*

- *The Enlightened Smoker's Guide to Quitting*

- *How to Help Your Smoker Quit*

- *Now Hiring* (with Steve Lauer)

A Wave of Thanks

And Other Human Gestures

31 Quick Stories

Bear Jack Gebhardt
Seven Traditions Press
Collins, Colorado

ISBN: 1938651065
Library of Congress Number: 2013915179
Printed in the United States of America

This one's for my kids,
Sam and Annalee…. Lights of my life
You're the best stories in the world.
I love you.

Stories

1.

A Wave of Thanks

"*O*h good," Bree Ann said out loud, though she was alone in her seven year old Subaru Forester. She was in the Whole Foods parking lot, looking for a parking space. She had just spotted an opening next to a new Chevrolet Suburban SUV where a petite blond woman was moving the last of her bags into the back seat.

Like most of the people now jamming the lot, Bree Ann had just gotten off work, hoping for a quick stop to pick up something for dinner. She had cell-phoned her son to let him know she'd be a tad late since she was stopping at the store, and was there anything he needed? Yes, more bananas, and they were out of sunflower seeds.

Bree Ann waited for the lady to clear her cart from the empty space. The lady, bleach blond, Bree Ann now saw, in tan pants and silky blouse, glanced at Bree Ann but pretended not to notice. She closed her door and then, instead of moving the cart out of the empty space, opened the driver's door and stepped up and closed the door.

"Hey!" Bree Ann said, out loud again, to no one again. She heard the Suburban engine come to life.

"Hey bitch!" Bree Ann said, not believing that this lady was going to leave her empty cart sitting in the middle of a perfectly good parking space.

The Suburban started to back out. Bree Ann slammed her hand on the horn, took her foot off the brake and pulled forward ten feet to block the lady from backing out, still pressing on the horn. People walking in and out of the store looked down the parking aisle at her.

The lady in the Suburban jerked to a stop. She looked over her shoulder, through the driver's window at Bree Ann.

Bree Ann pointed vigorously, eyebrows furled, at the shopping cart in the empty parking space. The lady in the suburban looked away and started inching back towards Bree Ann's Forester. Again, Bree Ann laid on the horn.

"Bitch!" she called out, though she knew the lady couldn't hear her. "What are you doing? Get the fucking cart!"

The lady in the Suburban inched further back.

"No!" Bree Ann said, shoving the gear shift into park and opening her door. She released her seat belt and angrily marched to the Suburban's driver's window.

"What are you doing?" Bree Ann yelled. "You can't just leave your cart in the middle of the parking space."

The blond lady wasn't looking at her. She was reaching down into the driver's door compartment. When she did look up she had transferred a small Colt pistol to her right hand and was pointing it at Bree Ann.

"Holy Jesus," Bree Ann said, immediately leaning back and backing away. The lady's automatic window rolled down.

"Move your fucking car," she said in a very calm voice, pointing the pistol. Bree Ann kept backing away, then suddenly turned and sprinted around the Toyota Camry which was parked next to the empty space. Bree Ann ducked down, then popped up.

"Move the cart, I move my car," Bree Ann said, and then ducked down again.

"Jesus H. Christ," the lady in the Suburban said, opening her door. She went to the cart and shoved it so hard that it hit the grill of a Toyota Corolla. She climbed back into her Suburban.

"Okay, okay," Bree Ann said, and sprinted around the Camry to her own car, with the driver's door still open. She climbed in, out of habit fastened her seat belt, and backed up, and continued backing up. The Suburban backed out, turned, and went in the other direction. When the Suburban disappeared, Bree Ann slowly approached and pulled quietly into the now empty space. Holding to the top of the steering wheel, she put her head on her hands.

She heard a car approaching. She looked and saw a white-haired woman in an Oldsmobile Cutlass hoping for a space. Bree Ann got out, got the bags from the back and grabbed the cart which was against the Toyota bumper. The white haired lady waved thanks.

2.

Morphic Resonance

"*I*'ll be out of the office tomorrow, Gladys, so here's my monthly report. I've footnoted the expenditures with a copy of my receipts so you can itemize how each was necessary and what line item it references for each of our projects."

Gladys, sitting at the front desk, was looking up at Dr. Weingarten, not aware that her mouth was hanging open. Dr. Weingarten's wide grin made his normally thin sunken cheeks puff out. He knew he'd surprised her, again.

"Thank you, Bruce," Gladys said, meekly.

"My pleasure," he said. "Just doing my job." He almost clicked his heels as he turned smoothly and went through the doors and disappeared.

"Something's really changed with that guy," Gladys turned and whispered to Belinda, her co-conspirator. "You think he's on drugs?"

"Definitely," Belinda responded. "And whatever he's on, I want some."

For the seven years he had been with the department, Dr. Bruce Weinstein was notorious for missing his monthly deadlines and quarterly summaries so necessary for grant administration and renewal. It had been Gladys' unhappy challenge to regularly coax and pry the reports from him.

"Some of us are actually too busy doing the real work," was always his irritated excuse.

Not only was this the second month in a row that he had turned in his reports ahead of deadline, he had also found time to repair a long-faulty drawer in one of the front desk filing cabinets, fix the leaky faucet in the sink in the break room and transplant two African violets wilting and overcrowded that had been sitting forlorn in the administrator's waiting room.

Gladys and Belinda were not the only ones who had noticed a change in his behavior.

"Bruce, my God, what have you done to your laboratory?" asked Dr. Murphy, the department chairman, one day in passing.

"Morphic resonance," Bruce replied with a smile. "Every form evolves towards its ideal."

"Don't give me that crap," Dr. Murphy said, obviously irritated. Bruce just shrugged, and grinned.

"Well, whatever it is, it looks good, even slightly professional, for a change." Dr. Murphy turned and continued on to his office.

Bruce Weinstein's small genetics lab had been notorious for its disarray. "Disarray" is generous. Total chaos was much more accurate. Old coffee cups on top of the mass spectrometer which was buried under journals and loose papers in no apparent order. Last year's test tubes and beakers shoved aside to make room for this year's new projects.

"Morphic resonance," Bruce repeated after Dr. Murphy had disappeared down the hallway.

"Explain it to me again," his wife Denise had begged. They were sitting on the newly-cleaned patio with a glass of wine and salmon on the grill. This was a different man from the one she had known the previous twelve years. This new man was clean, tidy, and very adept.

"The magical germ crawled out of the test tube and into my brain," he said, raising his glass to her.

"Bruce, quit talking in riddles. You've used that silly phrase before and I don't know what it means or what the hell you're talking about. Explain it to me again. What's happened to you?"

"Morphic resonance," Bruce said. "That's the germ of a magical idea that I saw in the test tube. I saw that the higher level field always modifies the probability structure of the lower level field."

"I don't get it," Denise said. "Talk plain English."

"Sorry Love, I really don't mean to be flippant. It has to do with hierarchal structures. Every form in the universe is part of a field, with an ideal form towards which it is moving, or evolving."

"English, Bruce, English," Denise said, taking another sip of her wine, studying him, truly wanting to understand.

"Okay, take our patio, Bruce said. "There's a living field here. We could call it a patio field. Our patio wants to express its own unique version of every patio that has ever existed."

"You've lost me."

Bruce drank from his own wine. "Okay, let's simplify. Take a stuck drawer in a filing cabinet. Because of morphic resonance..."

"What's morphic resonance?"

"It means higher form, or field, rules the lower form, or field, or at least influences it. Big fish eats the little fish."

"Okay, go ahead, but I don't know how this relates to a stuck filing cabinet drawer."

"The stuck drawer is a lower field. It actually wants to become unstuck, and act like the other drawers in the bigger field. Drawers are designed to function. There's an underlying harmony in the universe."

"The drawer wants to become unstuck?"

"Well, in a manner of speaking, yes. But we are human beings. The human being field is inherently a very high field. An incredibly higher order field. Just being present we influence our surroundings. So all outer forms and functions want to conform to the human field, or at least are willing to conform. The higher field influences the lower field. That's morphic resonance."

"Are you taking some kind of drug?" Denise interrupted. "The germ out of the test tube thing? Gives you energy? Makes you want to fix things? Did you cook something up there in your lab?"

Bruce gave a little laugh. "No, no, Love. Not at all. I just finally understood, at least a little, how things come into existence. They do it through morphic resonance."

"Sorry, but I just don't get it," Denise said. She took another sip of her wine, then held her glass back, studying it. "Where'd you get this stuff? This isn't what we generally drink, out of the box. This is really, really good."

Bruce looked at her, somewhat frightened, but understanding perfectly how it happened, simply being in his presence.

3.

Double Entanglements

The damned dog's leash got tangled around my one leg. I'd left my other leg at home because of an infection on my stump. So the damned dog also got tangled up around my crutch. Right leg. Left crutch. I would have used my right crutch to smack the mutt, but I was forced to hold the crutch firmly to the ground just to stay upright.

So okay, everyone asks, or wants to ask, howdja lose your leg? The answer is Fallujah. Can't blame folks for asking, wanting to know. They're just curious, maybe sympathetic and down deep want to know how to avoid losing their own damned leg. So my advice is, if you want to keep both your legs, stay out of Fallujah, God forgive us.

Better yet, stay out of the armies all together. Any army, any country. Even armies with different names, like navy, air force or marines. It's all army. Meaning arms, as in missiles, drones, hand guns, bayonets,and everything in between.

Without arms, you have no army, air force, navy or marines. The only purpose of arms is to take off legs. So don't play that game if you want to stand upright with both feet on the ground.

As you might tell, I have an attitude.

I was standing on the corner outside Starbucks when this chick's labradoodle-or whatever the hell you call them-some kind of mutt, comes zipping out at the end of one of those extended leashes, runs between my leg and my crutch, and then the chick calls, "Roscoe," or whatever the hell name he had, "no, no, bad dog, bad, come here." So Roscoe, being a good dog, turns around to go there by taking the hair pin curve around my leg.

"No, no, Roscoe," the lady says, starting to panic, running towards us. She wasn't the only one. Both Roscoe and me were getting jazzed.

The chick apparently had her leashy thing on lock because when she started running Roscoe suddenly had more string to work with. Not enough, apparently, to avoid confusion because after circling my leg he could tell something was wrong so he headed back in the other direction and circled my crutch. So now I could feel the mutt tugging on both my leg and my crutch. "Hey, hey, hey," I was shouting, wanting to lean down to grab him but couldn't.

"No, no, no, Roscoe," the lady was shouting.

All this happened—the dog running up, first circling my leg then circling my crutch, the young lady shouting, me shouting —all this took place in just a few seconds, much quicker than it's taking me tell you about it. Sort of like a bee sting. One moment you're good, everything's fine, the next moment you're in pain, absolutely not good. Sort of like Fallujah.

"I'm so, so sorry," the young girl said, coming up and kneeling down around my crutch and leg, reaching for Roscoe, trying to untangle the tangle.

"Careful, careful," I said. I could feel her reaching was making Roscoe tug even more on the crutch, which in turn pulled tighter on my leg.

"How in the world . . ." she said. "I'm so, so sorry."

"Here, here, let me help," said some young guy in a dark pony tail who happened to be passing by. He, too, crouched at my leg and crutch.

"Hold the dog," I said, hoping to ease the tugging.

"Yes, yes, here boy, here boy," the young guy said, grabbing Roscoe's collar and then, after a small struggle, undoing the clip. The tension immediately let up.

"Oh thank you. Yes, that helps," the young lady said. "I'm so, so sorry." She was finally able to unwind the now empty leash .

With the guy holding the dog by its collar, she stood up and faced me and put her hand lightly, briefly on my shoulder. "I'm so, so sorry," she said yet again.

"Life happens," I said, shrugging my shoulder.

"It was kind of funny," she said with a very quick smile. Again I shrugged and gave her a polite smile. She saw me not laughing.

"But not really, I know," she said. "It wasn't funny."

And then, going around me, turning to the young man holding her dog, she said, "I need to hook him back up."

"I think you need help with this big guy," the young man said. "Here, hand me the hook." She handed him the end of the leash to hook up her dog.

"Yes, thank you," she said to him. "I'm so sorry. I'm Heather. Thank you so much."

"I'm Jason," the guy said, standing up after getting Roscoe back on the leash. "I better walk with you a bit, make sure you two don't get into more trouble." Heather giggled.

As they walked away with Roscoe, she stopped, turned again and faced me. "Really, I'm so, so sorry," she said, a final time. "Is there anything I can do?"

I just shook my head. As they walked away, I heard the young guy say, "You were right. That really was kind of funny." Heather giggled.

Can't blame 'em. Life happens. Love happens. You laugh or you cry. I turned. Time for another cup of coffee.

The image of all three of them, *bam, bam, bam*, one after another, in my Fallujah sniper scope, was fleeting. I didn't dwell on it. I'm healing. Really.

I'm the cause of their meeting. I hope they hit it off.

4.

Understandably Not Talkative

Shortly after midnight Lonnie slowly raised the window, stuck his head inside, listened, looked. The window screen was on the ground beside him.

Stillness. The dining room table polished. Carved cherry wood chairs. The long buffet, with lace.

Lonnie pulled his head back out, reached for the small canvas duffel bag at his feet, looked around the darkened neighborhood. Nothing. Several blocks away, a dog barked twice then stopped. Then twice more.

Again Lonnie stuck his head in, listening, looking. He reached his arm through the window, placed his bag on the hardwood floor. He jumped himself up head first, halfway through the window, belt resting on the window ledge.

Suddenly, *thunk*! The window fell back down, pinning Lonnie half way in, halfway out, his legs kicking.

Virginia Claussen's eyes flew open. What was that? Sounds coming from downstairs. Definitely. She fumbled for the phone beside her bed. The oversize lighted numbers made it easy to call 911. "I think someone's in my house," she said, in a whisper.

Lonnie couldn't go forward and couldn't go back. His belt was caught in the metal molding of the heavy wood framed window. And from the inside, there was nothing for his arms to push against, no where to get leverage either forward or back.

"Oh geez," he muttered. "Geez. Geez. Geez."

Virginia Claussen put the phone on the nightstand without hanging up. The dispatcher had told her to please hold on, do not hang up. But she had to see what was going on. Her slippers, of course, were beside the bed, her cane beside the nightstand. Automatically, as she swung her legs off the bed, she slipped into her slippers and reached for her cane. She slow-stepped across the room, took her old worn bathrobe off the back of the door, put one arm, then the other into the robe, leaning her cane on her hip as she did. She slowly, quietly opened her bedroom door and started down the hall. Something was definitely going on downstairs.

Lonnie could hear the creak of the floorboards upstairs. He started to panic. He tried to turn sideways, but the old window was too heavy. There was nothing to push against to back out. He had to keep moving. The only way was forward. He scooted, wiggled, scooted some more, arms and legs waggling. Something gave.

Lonnie slid out of his pants, two feet further into the house, his hands now touching the floor, his legs still trapped at the knees by the heavy wood window frame.

As Virginia Claussen came into her living room she reached for and flipped the light switch. Lonnie, both hands on the floor, legs trapped by the window sill, bare buttocks aimed toward the ceiling, looked up, mouth open.

"I . . . I . . ." Lonnie started to say, but there was nothing to say.

"You naughty little whipper snapper," Virginia Claussen said, crossing the room, surprisingly quick. "What in the world . . ."

She let her sentence fall away and began to hit him repeatedly on his bare buttocks with her metal cane.

"Oww, no, oww," Lonnie muttered, and turned, trying to twist away.

"You have no right to be in here young man," Virginia Claussen said, still hitting.

Just then, two policemen appeared at the outside window. "Don't move," the policeman ordered, grabbing Lonnie by the ankles, where his pants had gathered. The suddenness of this frightened Lonnie such that he kicked, turned, twisted and then fell onto his back on the living room floor, his ankles caught by the window. His pants fell to the ground in front of the officers.

The judge sentenced Lonnie to three to five years in the state reformatory, after the charges of attempted rape had been plea-bargained down to breaking and entering and lewd and lascivious behavior.

On one occasion, Virgina Claussen took the bus out to visit him, to see how he was adjusting. After he apologized for what he had tried to do, they discovered they didn't have much to talk about, very little in common. It was awkward for them both. She didn't visit him again. Understandably, Lonnie had not been very talkative

5.

The Good Life

"What's this line for?" Larry asked the short wiry guy at the end of the line.

"Hell if I know. I heard they're asking people what they did with their lives," the short guy said.

Larry had been dead for three hours. Well, apparently not dead, because here he was standing in line. But three hours ago he'd been on the thirteenth hole at Fairview, having a decent round of golf with Charlie and Dave and a pick-up player named Finney. Larry had hit a pretty decent tee shot and was studying the layout for a nine iron approach to the par three green, when the pick-up player, Finney, walked over and nonchalantly said, "Okay Larry, time's up."

Finney had seemed a decent enough fellow, not too chatty, competent on the green-though no club pro-seemingly grateful to be included and playing with three old chums. Larry had not been taking any longer than usual in studying his shot, and certainly no longer than Dave normally took, which was forever.

"What do you mean, time's up?" Larry asked. "Not even my turn."

"Game over. Time's up."

"Game over?" Larry asked. "What the hell's that supposed to mean?"

Finney shrugged his shoulder, pointed palm out towards the near fairway. Larry looked where Finney was pointing and saw a commotion going on--- Dave and Charley and a guy who looked like Finney himself gathering around some fat old geezer down on the grass.

"What the hell's that?" Larry asked.

"You never knew what hit you," Finney said. "Matter of fact, you didn't even know you'd been hit. Dave's two shot."

Larry looked and recognized his own green leisure suit and new white tennies on the guy sprawled out on the grass. Other golfers from nearby were coming over. Dave was going spastic, blubbery. Charlie was on his knees, bent over. The guy who looked like Finney was on his cell phone.

"Your wish was granted," Finney said.

"My wish?"

"No nursing home. No big illness. No disability. How many times did you say you hoped to play golf 'till the day you died?"

"Yeah, yeah, that was my line," Larry admitted. "But I was just kidding. Some day. But I'm not ready. Not yet."

The next two hours—hours from Charlie and Dave's perspective—Finney stayed with Larry, explaining how hardly anyone is ever ready, as they watched the EMT's load his old body into the ambulance, heard the guys decide not to finish the round, and then the shock and tears of Alice, his wife, there in the hospital.

"I don't believe it, I just can't believe it," she kept repeating. And then she started calling, first her sister, then his sister, then friends of the family. "On the golf course he got hit on the head, right above his ear, with a golf ball. Apparently died instantly."

Larry asked Finney how he, Finney, could be both "over there," on the golf course with the guys, even calling 911, and "over here," with Larry, explaining what was happening. "I was sent to get you," Finney explained, though that didn't explain things so Larry could understand.

After several hours of watching the commotion, somehow moving between the golf course, the hospital and back to his own house on Clover Lane with Alice, Finney had led him here, to this long line in front of some kind of church or temple or government building where a wide variety of people were waiting, all looking a bit anxious.

"They're asking us what we did with our lives?" Larry asked the short, wiry guy wearing a baseball cap who was in front of him.

The guy shrugged. "That's what I heard."

Larry started considering his forty years as purchasing agent for Sports Inc., his long marriage to Alice, that time when he was young and slipped up with Katie, the receptionist, the big fight and then getting back together, his years since retirement, playing golf, traveling. Larry wondered what business it was of anybody else what he did with his life.

"Who's asking?" Larry asked the guy in front of him.

"I don't know," the short guy said, obviously a bit irritated. "I'm just as new here as you are."

"Maybe first I'll just go look around a little," Larry said, not necessarily liking what was happening at the end of this line. "Get the lay of the land. Save my place, okay?"

"They don't allow it," the little guy said.

Larry thought about it then shrugged his shoulders. "That's okay. I'm in no hurry. I'm going anyway, check things out."

He looked around. And then, pleasantly surprised, saw what maybe looked like a golf course in the green pasture distance. He headed in that direction.

6.

Coming and Going

Outside, Henry heard the car door slam. He quickly finished wiping off the counter and threw the sponge in the sink. He turned on the tea kettle sitting on the stove and turned off the radio, tuned to the local classical station. His mom and his Aunt Harriet had a hard time hearing when there was background music playing. They had a hard time hearing even when no music was playing.

He walked to the living room, looked out his picture window. He'd meet them, of course, on the porch or front walk. They were coming for Sunday lunch, again. He knew this was a short season in his own life, and he should be grateful. And he was. Neither of these women would be around forever. To be in a position to care for one's parents and older relatives in their last years was both a destiny and a privilege. Though sometimes a hassle, of course.

Preparing a brisket and sweet potato lunch, ready for these two after they'd been to church, was a relatively easy and mostly enjoyable affair. They would tire by two, and depart for their shared condo. They knew Henry liked to watch the Sunday football game.

Looking out the window, Henry's mind stopped. He looked, and looked again. His head jutted forward.

Coming up the walk, with mom and Aunt Harriet, was his Uncle Ralph, with his arm around Harriet. Impossible! He looked yet again. Yes, it was definitely him. The thin nose, the receding hair, the worried eyes. It wasn't a look-alike. It was Uncle Ralph himself, in his usual sports shirt and tan pants. No mistake. And yet, and yet . . .

Impossible! Uncle Ralph had died thirteen years ago. Henry, still married to Louise at the time, had gone to say his goodbye's, there in the hospital room. And then he'd helped with the funeral arrangements. But here was Uncle Ralph again , clear as day, with his arm around Aunt Harriet, coming up the walk.

Henry watched out the window to be sure. He looked for details. Yes, the clunky shoes. The big carpenter hands, the strong neck. No question: Uncle Ralph.

Henry left the front picture window and went to open the front door. His mind was on tilt, stuck, with no where to go. His heart was loud.

He opened the front door just as his mom and Aunt Harriet stepped on to the porch. No Uncle Ralph. Henry opened and held the screen door.

"Hi ... where's ... I just saw..." Henry started to say.

"Hi sweetie," his mom said.

"Henry, this is always so nice," Aunt Harriet said. "I so look forward to it." The two white-haired ladies, carrying their purses and dressed in church clothes, came in as Henry held the door.

"Smells good in here," his mom said.

"Let me take your coats," Henry said. "Aunt Harriet, you won't believe what I just saw. Or thought I saw."

"Oh?" Aunt Harriet said as Henry helped her out of her coat.

"Uncle Ralph," Henry said. "Clear as day, as you were coming up the walk. He had his arm around you. I saw him clear as I saw you. I swear."

"Oh that doesn't surprise me," Aunt Harriet said, without much emotion, moving to the couch and easing herself down. "He's always looking after me. And I was just thinking about him, as usual as we came up the walk, wishing he were here."

"Yea, but I actually saw him. . . saw him," Henry insisted.

"How nice," his mother said, removing her own coat. "What can I do to help?" She put her coat on the back of the chair she normally sat in and moved toward the kitchen.

That evening, his mother called in a panic. "Something's happened to Harriet. She just fell over, while we were watching TV. I couldn't wake her. I called 911. They're on their way. I think she's gone, Henry. I think she's gone."

"Okay, okay," Henry said. "I'm coming, I'm on my way."

7.

The Old Pole Vaulter

Albert sat in the shade of his small back patio, breathing softly while breaking bread into small chunks. Occasionally he tossed one of the chunks to the squirrels and sparrows gathered around the two feeders he kept filled with sunflower seeds just outside the patio. He himself didn't like white bread, but he'd buy a loaf every now and then because his critters, as he called them, seemed to prefer the white bread over the whole wheat or pumpernickel.

After his wife Thelma died, Albert realized she was the one who had all the friends. He had his own friends, of course. Pete, down at the barber shop; Larry, their insurance guy; and his best friend, Max, his partner for many years in the plumbing and heating supply business. But Max had remarried and Barbara, his new wife, liked to travel and spend time near her kids. Max wasn't around much any more. And when he was, Barbara kept him on a short leash.

After they sold the plumbing supply business, which he and Max had built over twenty-eight years, and where Thelma kept the books, he and Thelma traveled some, taking a few Viking

Cruises in the Caribbean and one Seniors Abroad trip. But then Thelma got her diagnosis and for several years they dealt with that, until the end. She had been the one who liked to travel. He could take it or leave it. With her gone now, he'd leave it, of course. A lot of trouble to travel. And a lot of expense, though he was grateful Thelma finally got to see at least a little of the world.

He and Thelma had two daughters who now had families of their own, one in Pittsburgh, the other in Seattle. Both daughters had encouraged Albert to move closer. He visits one or the other on holidays and keeps in touch by phone. But again, they have families of their own, friends of their own, lives of their own. They don't need to be regularly entertaining him. He doesn't want to be a burden.

Albert recognizes a few of the squirrels as regulars. Even recognizes a couple of the sparrows and house finches that frequent his feeders. He sometimes talks to them, encouraging them not to be so rude to their siblings, to be more willing to share. But mostly he doesn't talk. He just feeds, and watches.

Lately, sitting on the patio, for no reason he can fathom, Albert had been thinking more and more about his high school pole-vaulting career. It never was much of a career. He did take third place in one meet. That was his high point.

He told himself, both back then and now, that the reason he wasn't better was because he also had to work after school, first at the drug store and then at the auto-parts store. He couldn't spend as much time at the track, practicing like he should have, might have. But he went out all three years, sophomore, junior and senior, getting better each year, actually traveling with the team for away events, and when he was a senior, earning himself a letter and letter jacket.

Today, sitting on his back patio, Albert realized that memories of his pole vaulting had been coming up for three days in a row. What he particularly remembered was the feeling of steady, quiet tension and concentration necessary just before sprinting toward the bar, pole poised. When the moment was right he would start, picking up speed, running faster and faster down the approach, finally planting the pole, going up, up, his legs still kicking, pulling with his arms, turning toward the sky, up, up, at the last moment turning, lifting himself up over the bar, pushing the pole back, falling free through the air to the soft mats or straw on the other side.

Of course, most of the time he was not that good. On most of his runs he crashed through the bar with his body or he held on to the pole too long or he crashed through the bar with both his body and his pole. But sometimes, sometimes he did everything exactly right. His attention, his concentration, his approach and high lift, timed release and descent—all just exactly right. Ahh, that was the rush, the moment that made it all worthwhile.

Albert wondered why his youthful pole vaulting had been so much on his mind these last days. Then suddenly he felt it and recognized it —this tension, this expectation that had been building since Thelma had passed on—was curiously similar to that which he had felt just before sprinting down the approach track to lift himself high into the sky, over the bar.

Albert threw the last of the bread crumbs to the mama squirrel and baby squirrel shuffling seeds at the base of the feeder. He stood. He felt the tension and concentration of his body, just as it felt when he was in high school, though he was fifty pounds lighter back then. And yet in the same way, he now needed to move, he needed to rush, pull himself up, up, over the bar.

Albert turned, went back into his quiet house, shuffled through papers next to his easy chair, found the one he was looking for, went to the phone, dialed.

"Hi, Meals on Wheels? I see you're looking for volunteer drivers to deliver meals on Wednesdays. I could do that, I think."

8.

Evolution

I probably would have—or should have—left Damien a lot sooner than I did, except I have this cool photo tat, covering the whole front of my left thigh of Damien wearing his dark shades.

It's a new process they have—or at least new when I had it done—where they take a photograph and somehow get it in their computer so they can make it whatever size they want and then shine it to wherever you want to put it. Then the tattoo guy copies the photograph onto your leg, or wherever you want it. You have to go back a bunch of times and each time they have to get the photograph positioned exactly like the last time, but they're really good at it and in the end you have this really cool tattoo that looks almost exactly like a photograph. I did black and white. Color would have cost me crazy much. I was going to say it would have cost an arm and a leg but that would have been confusing since I'm talking about a tattoo on my leg.

At any rate, I have this tattoo that looks just like Damien that goes from a couple inches above my knee, where his neck and shoulders are, to almost the top of my thigh, with his long black hair and wearing his really dark sunglasses, so you can't see his eyes. It's a really cool tattoo and we used to have a blast walking around, me in my shorts or cut-offs, Damien in his shades, people would always do a double take, it was so obvious this was the guy in the tattoo. Probably it was the shades that made it so obvious.

Of course, later I find out that Damien's mostly a jerk. He won't grow up—or can't grow up, can't even hold a job. And wasn't all that faithful.

We have a kid, Stephanie, who is the whole world to me. She's nine now. I got the tat when she was sixteen months, which I probably should have known better even then. I just thought it would be cool for her to know how I'd committed myself for life--that's what tattoos are about: a commitment for life. I also wanted to freeze-frame a picture of Damien so she could see what he looked like when she was born.

My mom of course thought the tat was a stupid idea, a big mistake to begin with. She tried to talk me out of it once I told her what I was doing, after the first time I went. "It's not too late," she said, but it sort of was because they'd put in the outline. I figured she was only against it because she herself had a hard time staying with any guy for more than a few months, or a couple of years at most. Actually, okay, she's been with Max now for more than ten years and they seemed to have stuck it out together, through some pretty rough times, but when I was a kid it seemed mom had a new sleep-over almost every other week. Not quite that bad, but close.

Thinking back, maybe that's part of why I wanted the tat of Damien, up close and personal, on my thigh, to prove to myself and my mom and to little Steph that this was going to be a permanent thing that we could count on. I figured the tat showed that I wasn't the type of person to take this love thing lightly.

And then Damien turned out to be such a jerk, like I said. And, like I said, he couldn't hold a job, mostly because he's just lazy and wants other people to do the work, but he's also got an attitude, like he's too good to do the yucky stuff that his bosses ask him to do. And he's a jerk for other reasons that I won't go into.

At any rate, I stayed with him probably way too long, just because of that damned tattoo on my thigh. It's on the way front of my thigh, by the way, so don't get the wrong idea.

I checked to see how much it'd cost to get it removed, but it's way, way expensive, much, much more than it cost to put it on. My mom said she'd help pay for it but their Cutlass just blew a rod or something and they're as strapped for money as I am. It is something I'm going to have done one of these days, and I've already started saving a little, but I've got a long way to go.

I'm taking Damien to court again for past due child support. Child Services pays for most of the cost but it's still a real hassle. I've tried to figure out if I could just change the tattoo somehow so it didn't look like him, but I can't think of any way to do it.

Daryl, the guy I'm with now, looks a little bit like Damien so maybe if I could change the dark shades, and put in Daryl's eyes, but the guy at the tat place says the shades would be the hardest thing of all to change or remove.

I'm going to just wait, see how things work out. Besides, to tell you the truth, I'm not that crazy about Daryl. I'd hate to have his eyes following me around if we weren't still together. Janie Lee, my best friend, showed me how I might have the whole thing changed into a drawing of some monkeys climbing in a tree, with the sunglasses made into coconuts. That sounds stupid, I know, but it might be my best bet.

9.

No Bullets

"I think he's dead," Caleb said, kneeling down, looking at the big man laying on the floor behind the counter.

"Oh shit," Roxanne said, looking over Caleb's shoulder.

Moments before, they had walked into the Grab N Go convenience store wearing Roxanne's nylons over their heads and aiming their pistols—which they had, after long discussion, intentionally left empty, in case things went wrong. They didn't want to take the chance that this little venture could devolve into a tragedy they'd both regret.

They had waited in the dark in the alley across the street until there were no customers and the clerk was alone. Their old beater of a car was parked at the far end of the alley. The plan was to run in, do the deed, run back out, run to the far end of the alley, hop back into the darkened Chevette and continue on their way to L.A. They were both thinking, though mostly privately, that if this actually worked, actually brought in the two hundred bucks or so they needed for gas money to make it to the coast, then they just might try it again somewhere, further west, maybe collect enough cash to spring for a motel, a shower, real restaurant food. This was their first hold-up, but maybe they had a future.

"Freeze. Don't move. This is a hold-up, we need an extra bag," Caleb had said, almost according to plan, as he and Roxanne burst into the store. According to plan, Roxanne's job was, first of all, to try to look mean, tough, under her nylon mask, holding her pistol. Without the mask, she looked sixteen rather than nineteen, and, though a bit pudgy, innocent as an angel. Her next job, as Caleb was getting the money from the register, was to get chips and hot dogs from the hot dog turner, and whatever else that looked good that she could grab fast. They were both starved.

"I won't be able to carry it all while we're running down the alley," Roxanne said, thinking ahead.

"I'll get an extra bag," Caleb said. "And be sure to get mustard and relish."

The clerk was a short, fat man, in his early sixties, mostly bald except for a ring of stringy hair. He had a short, patchy, white whiskered unkempt beard. When Caleb and Roxanne came into the store, holding their pistols, his eyes got wide, his mouth dropped open, and then he grabbed his chest, grimaced in pain, said, "Aaaaa," and fell to the floor.

"Maybe he had a heart attack," Caleb said, kneeling down, leaning over the man. He pulled Roxanne's stocking off to get a better look. "I don't think he's breathing."

"Oh shit," Roxanne said again. "Maybe you should give him mouth to mouth, or call 911." She removed her own stocking.

"I ain't giving him mouth to mouth," Caleb said. "I ain't no homo."

"This isn't about homo," Roxanne said, slapping him on the shoulder, her nylon in her hand. "The man could die."

They both stared down at the man. Just then, the man's eyes fluttered and then opened. "Aaaaa," he said again, staring up at Caleb and Roxanne. They both jumped back.

"Don't shoot me," the fat man said, looking up at them.

"We can't," Caleb said. "We took the bullets out. We thought you were dead."

"Oh good," the man said, nodding his head, not moving from the floor. "I'm not dead. How much did you get?"

"We haven't got anything yet," Caleb said. The man nodded,

understanding, still not moving from the floor.

"How much do you need?" he asked.

"You're not dead? You're okay?" Roxanne asked.

"We're on empty and the yellow gas light just came on," Caleb said.

"Okay," the man said. "How about twenty five, and then you leave, okay?"

"It's not what we were hoping but that'd be great, and really help us out," Caleb said.

"Yes it would," Roxanne said.

"Okay, just a minute," the man said, and slowly rolled to his side and then up on his hands and knees, groaning softly. He let his head hang a moment. "You really scared me," he said, and then held on to the counter and gingerly pulled himself up.

"Sorry," Roxanne said.

The man moved slowly to the cash register. He looked at them both for a long moment. "You know, now that I'm thinking about it, I'll give you just fifteen," he said. He stood at the register, looking at them.

"You said twenty-five," Caleb whined.

"Yea, but I don't even know you and I'm feeling better now. And actually starting to feel a little bit pissed at this whole thing."

"Okay, okay," Roxanne said, pointing her pistol at the man. "Give us fifteen, and we'll be out of here."

"He said you don't have any bullets," the man said, looking at Roxanne and then nodding his head at Caleb.

"Maybe we do maybe we don't," Roxanne said. "Or maybe just he got rid of his bullets. You want to find out?"

"Not really," the man said. "I still don't feel so good." He pushed some buttons to open the register. He took out a twenty and a five, and then closed the register. "Here," he said, handing the bills to Roxanne.

"That'll do," Roxanne said.

"What about the hot dogs?" Caleb asked.

"Let's just go," Roxanne said, backing toward the door, still pointing her empty pistol at the clerk. "This isn't working."

"Okay," Caleb said, pointing his pistol at the cashier, and backing toward the door. "Don't move until we're gone."

"I won't," the cashier said. "But I still think you don't have any bullets."

"Maybe we should head back to Des Moines," Darryl said, back in the car, hoping for a nearby gas station. Roxanne nodded her head in the dark.

10.

Human Growth Hormone

"You're so short," were her first words when she opened the door.

My heart sank. I'd heard it before. "I started smoking at a very young age," I said.

After this introduction, for a long moment we both stood staring at each other. I was very worried she would say something not very nice and then simply close the door. Instead, she said, "You're Jeremy, right?"

"At your service."

"I'm sorry I said that," she said. "I was just . . .surprised."

"If I'm too short for you, we don't need to . . ." I let my words fall off. Actually, I didn't know what else to say.

"No, no," she said. "You're too short for anything . . . well, you know, real or personal, I mean anything permanent. Oh, what am I saying?"

I smiled and shrugged my shoulders.

"Well, you know, if you've already bought tickets and everything . . ."

I reached into my shirt pocket and pulled out two tickets and held them up for her to see.

"I'm sorry. I'm not saying anything right," she said. "I shouldn't have said . . .well. . ." And then she relaxed and smiled and my heart melted. She held out her hand. "Let's start over. Hi. I'm Rosalyn. You must be Jeremy."

"Yes, nice to finally meet you in person, Rosalyn," I said, shaking her hand, which was warm and soft and real.

"You were so funny in your e-mails and on the phone," she said. "And nice and smart and polite. I was expecting . . ."

"Someone taller."

"Sorry," she said. "Let's forget I said that." She blushed. She was beautiful.

"The jury will disregard all of the counselor's last statements and said statements will be stricken from the record"

For a moment, Rosalyn looked surprised and confused, and then broke into a wide grin again. And again my heart melted.

"See," she said. "You're funny."

47

Funny is about the only arrow I have in my quiver. When I stand up very straight—which of course I have learned to do—the top of my head just barely hits the five foot one inch mark. And speaking of heads, mine is much too big and hairy for the scrawny body to which it is attached. Twenty years ago, when the Lincoln County Foster Child Protection Services removed me from my step-mother's home—her prison—where I was kept mostly in my private, closet-like room and fed twice a day, they reported that although I was thirteen I had the physical stature of a seven year old. My schooling had been spotty, hit and miss, mostly miss. I had a lot of catching up to do.

"I guess I could have warned you," I said, still holding the tickets. "Not about being funny, but about being . . .well, being me."

"You are a strange looking little man," she said.

"And you are a very honest, open and observant woman," I replied.

"Do you still smoke?" she asked.

"Smoke?"

"Yes. You said you started young."

"Oh, right. No, I don't smoke. Never did. That's just a line I use."

"That's good," she said. "That would be a deal breaker."

"Wouldn't want to break the deal," I said. And then held the concert tickets up again. "This is the deal, right? You still game?"

"I'm still game," she smiled. "Let me get my purse."

●

Four and a half hours later, after the concert and desert, just before midnight, we were back in front of her door, saying goodnight.

"That was wonderful," she said. "Absolutely wonderful. I had a wonderful time."

"Wonderful," I replied. Again she laughed. We'd laughed a lot. And then she was quiet and looked at me a long moment.

"I'd like to kiss you," she said.

"Wonderful," I replied.

"Just a kiss. A goodnight kiss. To say thank you."

I looked up at her without responding. She slowly bent down, put her hand behind my head, and kissed me softly, tenderly on the lips.

And then she stood straight and it was over. "Thank you Jeremey," she said.

"I had a wonderful, wonderful evening. I'll need some time to think about it." She opened her door, stepped inside, turned, waved and closed the door.

That's how, walking home, I'd grown to measure six–foot-four.

11.

Larry's Night Cap

It was three in the morning. Larry's cell hummed on the nightstand next to his bed, indicating a text. He reached for it, held it close to his face. Couldn't read it.

Larry half sat-up, on an elbow, turned on the bedside lamp and reached for his glasses, held the cell again up close. The message was clear.

"We have received a message that your computer runs slow. Please call now."

"Uggh," Larry groaned, falling back on his pillow, still holding his phone, still wearing his glasses, the bed light still on.

Larry was driving to work. His cell phone rang. He checked and saw it was his boss. He swiped the phone with his thumb and held it to his ear. "Hello?"

"Yo, Johnson," his boss said. "Glad I caught ya. Listen, the Crenshaws are on their way in. You know old lady Crenshaw loves those pineapple turnovers from Potters Bakery, there on 23rd?"

Larry thought about it, searching for the right answer, but didn't have time.

"Would you pop over there on your way in and pick up a few of those babies? It'd be a nice surprise, a nice touch, especially if you could make it in before they got here. The Crenshaws are, after all, the Crenshaws."

"Okay, yeah, sure. I suppose so," Larry said.

"Good boy," his boss said. "And while you're there, might as well pick up an assorted bunch for the rest of us. Make sure you get some cinnamon. Petty cash will cover it, of course."

"Okay," Larry said.

"Great. See you soon, old boy. Don't dawdle. Crenshaws will be here at nine."

"Okay," Larry said, but it was too late. His cell indicated, "Call Ended."

That afternoon the subject line in one of his e-mails read, "Account Alert." He clicked. "You asked to be notified," the message read, "when your account balance went below . . .$300.00. Your account balance as of . . .2:19 p.m. . . .is now $89.73"

"Yeah, yeah, yeah," Larry said. "I know, I know. He realized Verizon's automatic bill pay had just sucked its monthly quart of blood.

On the way home Larry's cell phone rang again. It was his mother. She'd already left two voice mails. He should probably answer this one.

"Hi mom," he said, as cheery as he could muster. "What's happening?"

"Larry, Larry, Larry," she started, obviously upset.

Just then, with the phone to his ear, a flashing light caught his eye and he realized he'd just been caught on camera moments after that yellow light had turned bright red.

"Ah hell," Larry groaned.

"Larry!" his mother responded.

That night Larry was in his pajamas eating a bowl of ice cream in front of the television when the program was interrupted with loud beeps and an Emergency Alert about high winds and possible flash floods occurring three counties away. For some reason, the warning irked Larry. He hit the remote power button, turning off the television. He sat in his easy chair, holding the bowl, not lifting the spoon.

The sudden stillness of the room caught his attention. He could actually feel the stillness, like a comforting blanket. He sat contemplating the stillness for a long moment, hearing his own breath rising and falling in the stillness.

After what to Larry seemed a very long time, he again recognized the ice cream bowl in his lap. He lifted it, slowly moved it with its spoon back and forth in front of him. The movement of the ice cream bowl, he saw, did not affect the stillness of the room.

At that moment he suddenly realized that the stillness itself was quiet. These were two words—stillness and quiet—for the presence here in his room. He heard a car go by outside. The sound, he realized, did not interfere with the stillness and quietness, the quiet stillness that was here, that had been here all along. He set the bowl of ice cream down on the end table.

As Larry enjoyed the quiet stillness of the room-how the furniture just sat, not moving, the rug not talking--he recognized that the sound and movement of his own thinking likewise, did not interfere with the room's quiet stillness.

When Larry finally resumed his bowl of ice cream, now almost melted, the cool movement down his throat to the stillness in his stomach, appeared to him as the most wondrous stillness in motion he had experienced in many, many lifetimes.

12.

Tea, Take Two

Lin Tzu was blue-robed, his long pony tail neatly braided, clasped, showing his respect for our meeting. We sat.

I asked my attendant to prepare tea. Lin Tzu talked in the meantime about how he understood the teachings of the ancient sky mind texts. His speech was detailed, impassioned and illuminating. He had obviously studied for many years the five traditions and ten sects, and understood the subtle differences and similarities among them.

I had been looking forward to Lin Tzu's visit. He is a practical, well-educated scholar with a wide reputation throughout the Seven Provinces. I myself, so long confined to the monastery with those who, like me, had long been practicing sky-mind, most daily short conversations had become quite airy.

The tea was ready. I had sat without a word, listening, as if to evening birdsong, to Lin Tzu's profound renderings of our ancient wisdom. As Master of the Ceremony and elder of the clan it was now my honor and responsibility to pour the tea.

As all here know from sad experience, I am now at an advanced age, and my eyesight, as with other senses, is not as keen as once it was. As I poured tea, I was enraptured with his words about the mind being a cloudless sky in the timeless now while all forms and sensations appear and disappear within it. I was feeling, to be forthright, very spacey by his illuminating talk.

"Master!" Lin Tzu blurted out as I poured. "Please stop. The cup is full but you keep pouring."

I saw immediately what I had done. I feared he would see me as the doddering old fool I am, quickly losing touch with this meat-body realm. I had a position to uphold. I had not put anything away for retirement. Fortunately I was suddenly inspired with a great response.

"Like this cup, your mind is over-full of your own ideas and accumulated learning. If you want to learn something new, first you must empty your cup." This is of course true for tea-cups, but absolutely not true for this magical sky mind we all share at our root. Those who study the ancient texts do have many advantages, just as those who have acquired the vocabulary of wine tasting have thereby sharpened their senses to distinguish the subtle flavors, more so than those who lack the vocabulary.

I expected this to be Lin Tzu's response to my rudeness. Alas, he was in fact taken aback by my words, but then he lit up. He clasped his hands together and bowed.

"Thank you Master." He said. "I see the error of my ways."

I was disappointed that he had not seen through my ruse. So I was then forced to share my own understanding of this no-mind mind, just as I do every day with the other monks. Alas, that conversation between me and Lin Tzu became an over-worn beginner's teaching story in our community. I myself, however, now always wear my glasses.

13.

Beginner Bodhisattva

With the proverbial quiet little cat's feet, soft grey light snuck through the small, high-ceilinged north window of Ralston Clifford's cluttered studio apartment. Suddenly, with an electronic click, a loud man's voice came on, scaring the cat.

"Good morning Denver. Beware your early morning drive. We have a pile-up on Northbound I-25. . ."

Ralston, head down, pulled his legs up, scooched deeper under the covers. The news went on.

"A missing ten year old . . ." the radio voice complained.

Ralston, eyes now open, sighed, straightened his legs and pulled the covers away. He had intentionally moved the alarm to the top of his dresser, across the room, where he couldn't reach it from his bed. From experience he knew that if he could reach it, he'd stop it. And likewise from experience, he had turned the volume up.

Ralston swung his legs over the side of the bed and in the same movement—he'd learned he needed to keep moving or he'd allow himself to fall back into bed—he stood and lurched toward the dresser. On the way, his foot hit a ten pound barbell, stubbing his big toe.

"Ow, ow, ow," he said out loud, his first words of the day, as he hopped on one leg, holding his foot.

"Another armed robbery on East Colfax has merchants . . ." Ralston slammed his hand onto the snooze alarm. The radio went silent.

"Jesus," Ralston said out loud again with a spontaneous deep release of breath. Standing delicately on his injured foot, he fiddled with the radio. It came back on.

"Legislators are preparing for a battle over . . ."

And he turned the radio off again, not just snooze this time, but off off. In his plaid boxer length pajama bottoms he hobbled across the room to the chair next to the small kitchen table in his dinette. He sat, gently probed his sore toe. Flinched when he pushed it wrong. "Ow, ow, ow," he said again and let his leg down to the floor. He put both elbows on the newspapers covering the table. He closed his eyes. He realized he could easily go back to sleep right here, his head leaning on the palms of his hand.

He forced himself to open his eyes, staring down at the paper on the table. The headline read, "Morgues overflow in Syria." Ralston closed his eyes again.

He brought his attention to his breath. "One, one, one, one," he forced himself to think, watching the in-breath. "One, one, one, one," he thought again, on the outbreath. "Two, two, two, two," he thought on the next in-breath. "Two, two, two, two," repeated on the out breath.

He stood and moved toward the sink. "Three, three, three, three," he thought on the next in-breath. "Where'd I put the coffee I bought?" Three, three, three, three.

Last week he'd gone to a beginners meditation class with Theresa, a new girl who had moved into a two bedroom on the third floor. He went, at her invitation, not so much because he was interested in meditation, though he had been sort of curious, but more because he was interested in Theresa.

The instructor said one should meditate first thing in the morning, to set the tone of the day, to align the energies, bring peace and calm to one's self and thus the world.

"No matter how many beings there are in the universe," Ralston repeated the words of the instructor quietly out loud as he filled the coffee maker. "May they all be happy."

14.

Mortal Sins

When Father Andrew turned the corner from the parish house and started down the hill on his morning walk to the church, he saw that at the far end of the block he would have to walk around an old faded blue Plymouth that someone had parked across the walk, next to the curb, blocking the public right of way. His immediate, spontaneous inner response was a silent, yet vehement, "asshole!"

The spring morning was pristine. The air cool, but not cold. The purple rhododendrons and pink azaleas in full bloom. His quite recent bedroom prayers and meditations at the parish house had been deep, sweet and peaceable. Perhaps it was because his mind was so clear, at ease, his heart untroubled, that this unconscious, unsolicited "asshole" response caught his attention.

"Forgive me Father, for I have sinned," he mumbled to himself as he quickly and, he hoped, unobtrusively made the sign of the cross. "I have held enmity against my brother."

The little gesture was more a matter of mechanics and habit than of true repentance. He assumed the Plymouth probably belonged to some college kid who came home late, maybe a little buzzed, and could not find a real parking space along the crowded street. Rather than devote more time and effort to finding a space, the kid had simply parked, blocking the walk. Illegal, of course, but the punk had obviously decided he'd chance a parking ticket. Or maybe he was so drunk he didn't realize or didn't care he was illegally blocking the public walk.

"Asshole," Father Andrew thought again, this time more intentionally, more personally as he walked around the Plymouth, into the street and back, then resumed his walk toward the church.

Of course, Father Andrew knew he was a sinner. His own very human, very masculine, very Neanderthal response to people and events did not surprise him. His chosen profession—or was he chosen for this profession?—was not because of his purity. On the contrary, he had become a priest to help balance his all too obvious, at least to him, proclivities to violence, greed, self-aggrandizement. The holy institution had helped him grow beyond, or at least loosen the grip, of these impulses rising from his fallen nature.

Still, his morning's spontaneous "asshole" response to the parked Plymouth intrigued him. Before turning the corner he had been feeling deeply at peace, buoyant, happy with the world and his place in it. And then suddenly, this immediate and ragged condemnation of a fellow human being—a complete stranger to whom he could not even put a face— took over his mind because of a very minor infraction of social propriety. Granted, his was a momentary, fleeting response and perhaps of small significance in the larger scheme of things, yet it was quite obvious to Father Andrew that the "asshole" response, at least the first one, was completely involuntary on his part. Where had it come from?

When Father Andrew walked up the front steps and through the double doors of the church, his secretary, Glenda, immediately called out, "Watch out, Father, he has a gun!"

Andrew turned and saw Charlie Winters, the husband of Kathleen Winters, who had come to him with confession of her long-ago infidelities, and her husband's ongoing, almost insane jealousy.

"Okay, asshole," Charlie said. "Your time's up." Perhaps if he had used any other word, Father Andrew would not have spontaneously laughed. It was the spontaneous laugh, Charlie later told the police, that convinced him Father Andrew was indeed guilty, and had to die.

15.

RELAPSE

"Hey, Dr. John, listen, sorry to say, I shouldn't be spokesman for you guys anymore."

John Albert Flanagan, Ph.D., M.P.H., was taking the phone call at his large walnut desk in his private office on the third floor, the one with a large window overlooking a long lawn sloping down to the river. He had a more modest "working office" on the first floor where he saw clients.

"Why? What's happening?" Dr. John asked, though he had a sinking feeling that he already knew.

"You need to stop running those TV things, you know, with me in 'em."

"Danny, what's happening?" Dr. John asked. "You know we do have your written permission, and you've been paid . . ."

"Fell off the wagon, doc, sorry to say, six months or so ago. Just a few at first, but I'm back up to almost a pack a day again."

"Danny, why didn't you . . ."

"Thought I could stop on my own. You guys really did teach me, gave me some great tools . . ."

"Danny, let's don't give up. Why don't you just come in again, no charge, we'll...."

"No, doc, that's why I'm calling. I'm not ready to do that yet. Maybe later. Right now I just feel embarrassed to have those damned things going on TV."

"So what happened?" Dr. John asked, though he didn't really care. He'd heard so many stories like this.

"I went to a family reunion," Danny began. "I think I told you my whole damned family smokes . . ."

Danny explained how he had started with a single smoke with his favorite cousin and then another one later with his uncle and how now even though he had tried a lot of different things he was up to almost a pack a day and just didn't have the energy or the time to do the program again just yet. As Danny talked, Dr. John was pulling up Danny's client chart on his computer at the side of his desk.

"I think those commercials with me bragging about quitting and how easy it was, is making it even harder to quit," Danny said. "I think you guys should pull 'em for a while. I know my contract says I have to give back some of the money, and I will, if I don't quit, or when I get working again."

"Okay, Danny, sure. I understand. No problem . We have lots of other folks wanting to be in those commercials. We'll stop running them as soon as we can. We do have a contract, however, with the station that obligates us . . ."

"I've been tempted to go down to that damned station and tell them myself why they need to stop running them. Seeing myself grinning like an idiot saying how free I feel, I can't take . . ."

"No, no, that won't be necessary," Dr. John said quickly. "Don't do that. We may not even need the money back, if I just quietly sent you your contract."

"Hey, that'd be cool," Danny said. Dr. John looked at his computer.

"Are you still at 1738 Riverside, apartment six?"

"Yeah, yeah. Still here," Danny said. "Can't afford to move."

"Okay, great," Dr. John said. "We'll pull the commercials as soon as we can, and I'll even send you your contract back."

"Wow, that's great," Danny said. "This is working out even better than I thought. Better than me going to the station."

"It is, Danny, it is. You did the right thing."

"I knew you guys would want me to come back in. I'm just not . . ."

"No, no. No need to explain. I know how these things are."

"Thanks doc. That's great. Much better, much easier than I thought it was going to be."

After they hung up, Dr. John sighed heavily and turned slowly in his chair to look at the river. They actually didn't have a lot of people lined up to take Danny's place. Nor did they have other commercials, older commercials that they might substitute. Danny had not been the first spokesperson to fall off the wagon. Seems like this program works well for many people for six months, sometimes more, and then . . .

Everything would be much simpler, Dr. John thought, if Danny were dead. Had an accident. Or was shot by an intruder. No, no, that would be crazy.

Dr. John swung his chair back around, holding his head, resting his elbows on the desk, staring, thinking. Danny's commercial was the lifeblood of this clinic. And the blood was slowly draining--- fewer and fewer clients were coming, and the overhead was climbing. And the failing clinic had made his home life miserable. Diane was ready to leave him, even with the commercials running.

Dr. John stood up. He needed to take a walk, clear his head. It was crazy thinking, he knew, to even consider, like he was doing now, how to be rid of Danny permanently.

Walking the path by the river, he saw the Walgreen's store. He was surprised at the way his body moved in that direction.

"No, no," he said to himself. "This is absolutely insane."

"What the hell are you doing," a voice inside his head screamed. "It's been fifteen years . . ."

"A pack of Marlboro Reds, please," Dr. John said to the clerk. "And a lighter."

The clerk thought nothing of it, ringing up the sale.

Walking out, pulling the little red string opening the pack, Dr. John wondered if that same Walgreens might also sell handguns.

16.

Like People

"Maybe because I just don't like people, okay?"

Darrien's mom had just asked him, again, why on earth he had quit the chess club at Martha Trimble Middle School. It was Thursday afternoon, chess club day.

For the past week Darrien had been secretly trying out his new, "I don't like people" philosophy, but this was the first time he had spoken it aloud to anyone. He was somewhat surprised, and pleased, that his mom looked shocked. But she looked shocked a lot these days.

"Darrien, how can you say you don't like people?" she asked.

"Because maybe it's true," he said.

"I don't believe it."

"Believe what you want," Darrien said, and started to walk out of the kitchen but saw that tears had come to his mom's eyes as she studied him.

"Oh mom," he said, "don't take it so personal."

"But honey . . ." she started to say.

"That's just the way I am. It's not your fault."

"How can you not like people?" she asked. "You're people. I'm people."

"I just don't like people in general. I like you. It's just people I don't like."

Again, Darrien was somewhat surprised, and pleased that he had found an argument, a philosophy that was so hard to argue against and had so much impact. He had been exploring and playing with this "I don't like people" philosophy ever since he'd overheard Ralph Wingate's older sister, Vivian, say it to some guy she knew at the City Park bandstand who was bugging her about not hanging out.

"Nothing personal, I just don't like people," she had told the guy.

He had laughed a mean laugh. "Oh, I get it. You bat for the other team," he said. "You don't like guys. You're one of those . . ."

"No, you don't get it," she had come right back at him. "I like some guys and I like some girls but I just don't like people in general. Are you going to try to change me?"

The guy held up both hands, as if in surrender, and started backing away. "No, no," he said. "That's your privilege. You don't like people, far be it from me . . ." Then he shook his head and turned and walked away.

When the guy left, Vivian had turned and grinned to her friend and they both giggled.

"What a dork," her friend had said.

When he witnessed this Darrien thought that Vivian had been kind of rude to the guy, but Darrien had never heard anybody ever say they didn't like people, people in general. He didn't know that was allowed.

Darrien knew there were some people you liked and some you didn't like, but not liking people in general was a freedom, an attitude, he had never considered. The thought stayed with him. The more he thought about it, the more he liked it. Not liking people in general took a lot of the pressure off. You didn't have to worry about what people in general were thinking about you or what they expected. You could just do your own thing, and not worry about other people. Your own world would be what was important. Darrien liked that.

Until now, when he said it to his mom, he hadn't actually told anybody about his new philosophy. He hadn't officially quit the chess club, like he'd told his mom. He just didn't go to this week's after-school meet-up. He was practicing not liking people, not caring what they thought, and doing his own thing.

Darrien actually liked chess and was pretty good at it. In fact, he was one of the top two or three players in the club, which had a dozen or so members. He wasn't the best player. He had never beat Hamid, the kid from Iran. But he could sometimes give Hamid a run for his money, unlike most of the kids. People would sometimes gather to watch him and Hamid play.

Darrien's cell phone rang. It was Ralph, from the chess club.

"Hey Darrien, guess what, bro?" Ralph said, excited. Ralph was Darrien's best friend, but since it was Ralph's older sister who gave him the idea of not liking people, and since Ralph was there when they had both heard her say it, he couldn't tell Ralph about his new philosophy, since Ralph would know where he stole it.

"You've been elected president, bro," Ralph said.

"What?"

"Cindy Mortison is transferring next week. Her dad got some kind of promotion. So Mr. Birchfield said we had to elect another president, this week, since year book is going to be printed. You're going to be in the yearbook, as president. I nominated you. Burgs nominated Larry Spinsky, who was actually at the meeting, but you won, seven to three."

"Spinsky's a butt-head, and can't play chess worth piss," Darrien said.

"That's why you won," Ralph said. "I don't know where you were today, but you're our new Prez. That's what it'll say in the yearbook."

Darrien nodded his head, smiling, not saying anything out loud. Some people were pretty good sometimes.

Where Two or Three
Are Gathered Together

The police van idled in the brick courtyard behind the Lincoln County jail. Inside, two guards drank coffee from Styrofoam cups, laughing with the day clerk, waiting next orders.

"Jesus loves you, man," Peter Nessman said to Victor Scruggs, inside the van. "Just trust him. He'll take you through."

Victor, the shorter, squatter of the two, looked at Peter and stared. "Bullshit," Victor finally replied in a low, no-nonsense voice, still staring straight at him.

Peter and Victor were each in leg irons and handcuffed to iron rings in the back of the police van to be transported to the Lincoln County Courthouse for sentencing, each in a different courtroom, at separate times, for their separate crimes.

Peter sat up straighter, raised his eyebrows and leaned back on his bench. His hair was neatly combed, his jumpsuit somehow tidier. "No offense, man," Peter said. "Just trying to help."

Victor looked back down at the floor. Peter, younger than Victor, watched him closely. "I'll pray for you, brother," Peter said quietly, "that you might feel His grace, and find your salvation."

"Get your fucking hands off me," a lady's voice shouted as the back door of the jail opened and the two officers who had been drinking coffee and a third female guard brought out a small woman dressed in county overalls. She, too, was handcuffed and in leg irons. A fourth officer came through the back door of the jail and opened the back of the van. The three officers moved the screaming lady toward the van.

"I'm not going," she shouted. "I fired that fucking lawyer. You can't make me."

"Tell it to the judge, Dora," the lady police officer said, pushing her toward the rear of the van. The woman in cuffs pushed back, sank back, struggling, her chained feet out front. "No, I won't go. You fuckers . . .you can't make me.   I know my rights. I don't have to go."

"Dora, Dora," the lady police officer said, muscling her up and towards the van. "Don't give us trouble. We don't have a choice. You don't have a choice."

"I don't have to," she yelled again, trying to break free. The big officer next to the back van door stepped forward and kicked the woman's legs out from under her. She fell back into the three officers hands.

"Dora," the man who kicked her said. "If you don't behave, I'm going to send for Dr. Schmit. Give you another shot to calm you down."

Dora, regaining her feet, spat towards him.

"You bitch," he said, jumping back.

"You prick," she replied.

With an officer on each arm and leg, they managed to get Dora, still screaming, into the back of the van, managed to get her leg irons chained to the floor, her hands in handcuffs, behind her, locked to the back wall. She fought all the way.

"You fuckers," she yelled, one last time when they finally closed the door. "I know my rights." She was breathing heavily from the struggle when she finally turned to look at Victor and Peter.

"What are you assholes staring at?" she asked.

Peter shook his head and looked away towards the front of the van where the two officers were getting in, still talking with the others about meeting down at the courthouse.

"So tell her," Victor said, looking over at Peter. "What you just told me."

Peter shook his head quickly, slightly, not looking at Dora, and only quickly at Victor. He furled his eyebrows, wanting Victor to be quiet.

"No, go ahead, asshole," Victor said. "Tell her how Jesus loves her."

Again, Peter shook his head quickly, looking away.

"Oh yeah," Dora said, "That's all I need right now." And then she started crying, deep, deep sobs.

"Sorry sister," Victor said softly, when she slowed down and caught her breath. "It's the shits, I know."

"Nobody understands," Dora said. "Nobody listens. Nobody. Nobody."

"I can dig it," Victor said. If he hadn't been chained to the wall, he would have reached out and patted this small stranger on the shoulder.

18.

Nun Rituals

By the time Hanna gets home from work at the post office, she's ready to be a nun. By then, she needs a gentler, more cloistered, even renunciate type of lifestyle.

"Our home should be our sacred retreat," she said to Darcy, her fifteen year old daughter. "When we come here, we need to feel we've reached safe ground, home ground. We need to be welcomed, or at least acknowledged. It's like we've just returned home from the wars."

"Yeah, right," Darcy said. "Was just watching my shows, mom. So what's the big deal? That I didn't call upstairs, hi mom? Welcome home?"

"Yeah. I guess that's it. When you don't interrupt your media for even a minute, what it means is that Everybody Loves Raymond, or whatever you were watching..."

"Real Killers..."

"Ok, what it means is that you've decided that Real Killers is more important than real people. Flesh and blood people."

"Okay, okay, mom," Darcy said. "I admit you're real. But Real Killers, you yourself have to admit, can be a lot more interesting than a mom you see every day."

Hanna laughed. "Yes, probably. Though it might depend on how hungry you are."

"How hungry? What do you mean?"

"Well, let's pretend you hadn't eaten in three days, and I just came home with a slab of bacon and a loaf of bread."

"I was eating a burrito when you came in."

"Yes, I know, but if you hadn't been eating a burrito, and you were real hungry, then you'd be happy to see me, right?"

"Okay. I'm happy to see you, mom. Welcome home from the wars. Thanks for bringing home the bacon. Now will you turn the TV back on?"

"Sure. Be happy to."

"You're weird, you know that, mom?"

"Yes, child, I do."

"Ok. Can I get back to my program now?"

"Yes, you can. I will pray for the good guys to win."

"That's weird, mom," Darcy said as she went back down stairs and Hanna went back out to the garage and flipped the breaker switch back to 'on.' From that day forward, Darcy yells, "Hi mom. Thanks for being home from the wars. Please don't flip the breaker switch."

It makes Hanna smile, just to hear it. She answers Darcy kindly, then goes upstairs and changes into her at home clothes, her habit, pleased with her young nun in training downstairs. Nuns do have their rituals.

19.

No Donuts in Forever

"Holy shit, is that Paul?" Rhonda's heart quivered.

She had just put two cans of Dole's crushed pineapple into her cart when she'd glanced to the far end of the grocery aisle and saw him. The recognition was there, her heart had quivered and her breath jumped into her throat then stopped.

Was it him? Yes. She knew it. No mistake. The quivering turned into racing.

"Mom can we get these?" Ten year old Max held up a package of star-shaped macaroni. "I like 'em."

Rhonda glanced at the package. "No, no" she said, out of habit, waving her hand. "Put them back."

The skinny blond-haired boy did put them back, without argument. He was not that invested in star-shaped macaroni. He started down the aisle, on the lookout for food treasures he might be willing to fight for.

"No, no, we don't need anything up there. Let's go back this way," Rhonda said, turning her cart around. Paul—she knew it was Paul, it had to be Paul— had passed this aisle pushing a cart toward the other end of the store, toward the fresh fruits and vegetables. Rhonda and Max had already been there, thank God. He hadn't looked her way, down this aisle, she was almost positive. She headed toward the bread and bakery.

"What is he doing here?" The question was so clear and simple and loud in her head she was almost afraid Max could hear it. "I'm seven years, three months clean and sober," was the next thought, which she almost said out loud.

"Mom, mom, we haven't had donuts in forever. You never let me. Forever and forever. Can I have one? Just one? Please, please, please?"

Max was holding on to the cart with both hands, shaking it softly as they walked. They were at the end of the aisle, moving on, past the rotisserie chicken.

Rhonda glanced quickly toward the other end of the store.

"Okay," she said. "Just one. Be sure to use a tissue. Don't use your hands. And put it in a bag."

"I will, I will," Max said, tearing off toward the donut case.

Again Rhonda glanced toward the other end. No sign of him. That's good. Maybe she'd duck down the frozen foods aisle. Her heart was slowing, but her breath was still ragged.

# # #

"Jesus H. That's Rhonda." Paul's heart felt a quiver. He looked quickly away from the canned fruit aisle. "That was her, I know it. Jesus H. Jesus H." To himself, of course, reacting.

Fortunately, she didn't see him. He was pretty sure. Almost positive. He quickened his pace. And the boy was with her. He wouldn't recognize him. Couldn't recognize him, even if he did see him.

Paul's heart continued to beat hard and his breath was ragged. "That which I have most feared has come upon me," he thought to himself, repeating a scripture he had learned in prison Bible study.

This is not the right time or right place, he thought. Maybe some time, some place, maybe it was inevitable. But with other people around. He and Rhonda would shake hands. Maybe her husband would be there, if she had one. And Paul would be with Lucinda, or maybe someone a little classier. Some place more formal. Maybe even intentional, with lawyers, they'd work out something, payments maybe or something, relative to the boy. But not here. Not like this, so soon after release. He just wasn't ready. Maybe he'd never be ready.

Moving quickly toward the far end of the store, Paul turned into the paper goods aisle. He and Lucinda, whom he'd dropped off at Walgreens, would need some paper towels. He had the rotisserie chicken in his cart. Maybe find some chips, and Lucinda wanted some fruit, then he could slip away, out of here.

Of all the grocery stores in a city with millions of people, what are the chances, just passing through, that he'd pick just this store, at just this time, when Rhonda and the boy, his boy. . .

Paul stood in front of the paper towels, closed his eyes, took a deep breath. And then another deep breath. His eyes still closed.

#   #   #

Rhonda stared at the frozen chicken dinners, not really seeing them. She wished for a brief moment she was still married to Barnett, and that he was here, right here, so Paul could see. She had a new life, really . . .

"I got one," Max said, coming up to the cart, holding up the small white bag with a single donut in it. "We can share, if you want. I didn't get my chocolate glazed, I got your cinnamon, your favorite."

Max wondered why that would make tears suddenly come to his mama's eyes.

20.

Lifting the Weight

"Mom, Mathew says when you get to heaven, you won't still be married to dad."

The cloudy blue eyes of the shrunken woman on the bed were already too big for her face, but these same eyes grew larger, wider, staring fearfully up at her silver-haired son. He sat on a folding chair by her bed, holding her hand. He wanted his words to sink in, hopefully in past the morphine. A small electric fan which he had brought for her months before sat on a dresser near the top of her bed and swept slowly back and forth regularly ruffling thin wisps of her unwashed hair. The nursing home had no air conditioning.

"No... yes," she slowly uttered, with long pauses. "... your father, he ...William, he ... we're married ... yes ... no..."

She was actually more cogent than her words revealed. It was the huge load of drugs that, at points during the day, made the words all sluggish, mixed up.

"You'll still be able to see him and love him if you want, and be with him, if that's what you want to do. But the Bible says you won't be married any more. You're finished with that. Done with that. You did good, mom. You did your job. But that's over now. The Bible says people neither marry nor are given to marriage in heaven."

She stared at him still with wide eyes. "No....We're still... yes, no... "

"You'll be married to Jesus..."

"Oh phooey," she said, quite clearly, emphatically. Her son laughed.

"Well, in some way you'll probably be married to Jesus. But the point is, you won't be married to dad anymore. You don't have to worry about that. You did that already. It's over."

She bit her thin dry lip. The fear in her eyes slowly changed into tears, of pain, sorrow, melancholy. He patted her hand. She understood what he was saying. "Really mom. You did good. But you don't have to worry about that any more. When you get to heaven, when you see dad, Jesus will be there, so all you have to do with dad is wave to each other, be glad to see each other, but you might not even have a chance to talk to dad. Jesus has a separate place for each of you. You will each have your own path, your own work. Dad will have different work than you. A different place. And you will have a different place than dad. Different friends. You can love and hug him, if you want, but you don't need to if you don't want to. You won't be married any more. That was only for here. That's what the Bible says. You'll have different adventures when you leave here. Dad probably won't be part of them. You don't have to worry."

"Really?" she asked, squeezing his hand. "You think?"

"Yes mom, really. It's over. Done, as far as you and dad are concerned. Not the love. Not the friendship. Not the laughter. That's not over. That will never be over. But your marriage vows. The responsibilities. The hurts. You did those already. No more marriage when you get to heaven. You'll just be friends."

She squeezed his hand again, and closed her eyes, again. He took a deep breath and let it out slowly. She breathed in fits and starts, the breathing of drugged sleep, although it started now, to ease.

"He was an asshole," he whispered, just below his breath. "You won't have to put up with that asshole ever again."

William Senior had been dead for twenty years. Even as he lay dying of cancer he had tried to hide from her a last note from one of his secret ladies. And now here he was again, messing with their lives, bringing her pain, again. The asshole.

His mom had been trying to die, ready to die, for over nine months. The stroke, the blood pressure, the congestion, the infections . . . none of these had been enough. She was holding on, holding back, not willing to let go. The doctors and nurses were baffled. Her other kids, William's brothers and sisters, and the grandkids had all flown in, had said their last good-byes and flown back out. And then flown in again, and back out. Still, she held on.

Last night, as he lay alone in the dark in his own bed, thinking of her wasting away in that place, he finally realized what it was that she, a woman of deep, unwavering faith for over eighty years, was so frightened about. He realized why she couldn't let go. She didn't want to see him again. Was afraid to see him again.

He patted her arm and removed his hand. She slept. After she had been in this place for a while, and it became clear she wouldn't be leaving, they had hung family pictures up on the wall next to her bed. Now, as she was sleeping, he leaned over and gently unhooked the picture of his dad as a young man in his army uniform. Holding the photo, he looked around the room and saw, leaning at the back of the sink, a sentimental painting of a field of blue bonnets. He retrieved the painting and hung it where his dad's photo had been. He leaned down and kissed his mom on the forehead.

"I'll see you in the morning," he whispered. "As usual. Sleep easy."

Her breathing softened as he left the room, the picture in his hand. The call came the next morning.

The Monkey Wrench

"Dad, I hate to throw a monkey wrench into everything, but . . ." there was a pause. "I don't think you ought to come right now. Now's not a good time."

Wilbur's heart dropped at the words. He held his cell away from his ear, closed his eyes and let out a deep breath. But he could hear his son's voice still talking. He brought the phone close again.

"It's just that, well, ever since the baby, Heather and I have had to work some things out. I'm pretty sure everything will be okay, but just right now, with the baby and all . . ." His son's words trailed off.

"Just now your crazy old man on your doorstep might upset the apple cart?"

"Yea. Sorta. Well, actually, exactly." His son laughed, but sounded sheepish.

"No, no, that's okay. I understand completely," Wilbur said. "We'll just postpone. A week or two. Or a month or two, if that would be better."

"Well, probably a month would be better," his son said. "Heather and I . . .well, it's been kind of rough for a while, especially with the baby, so until we get use to her, it might take us some time . . ."

"Sure, sure. I completely understand, as you might guess." It had been twenty years since Wilbur and his son's mother had divorced.

"Sorry to put a monkey wrench into things, here at the last minute, after we'd planned . . ."

"No, no, I understand. Really. Let's just postpone. I'm still coming out. I really do want to see that little princess, and your own ugly mug. Maybe drown some worms. Buy you a brewskie, give you a cigar. But we can do that in a month or two, just as easy. No prob. No biggie. I'll just rearrange."

"Really?"

"Yeah, really. Later would probably be better for me, too. Let's just figure July or August."

"Yeah, if that's okay. That would be great. Thanks," his son said, obviously relieved. "Let's count on July or August. Maybe August. I really do appreciate you, pop. You're the greatest."

"Yeah, yeah. Let's don't get fuzzy. You go. Take care of business. I hear that little lady squawking. We'll stay in touch, figure out the best time."

"You sure this doesn't goof things up completely for you? You've probably already got your vacation going and all. And I know you want to see little Priscilla. She's wonderful. You could still come out, it's just that . . ."

"No, no. This probably works better for me too. I'll just tweak some things at work. No biggie. Really."

"Okay. Thanks dad. I better run. I hate to do this to you."

"No, no. Like I said, probably be better for me, too. You go. We'll talk."

"Okay. I better go. Bye pops. Love ya. See you soon."

"Love you too, bud. Adios, amigo. Be kind."

"I will."

And with that, the call ended.

Still holding the phone, Wilbur looked at his suitcase sitting at the front door, next to three bags of baby items. They'd been sitting there for two days. He had felt silly, packing it all so early. He was just so ready, so excited about being with his son again, and seeing, maybe holding . . .

He sat down in his easy chair, silent phone in hand. Tears welled up. Two days ago he had gone to the post office to put a hold on his mail. The thought of starting it back up again broke his heart. And at work, he had promised he'd bring back pictures.

"Angie," he suddenly said out loud, in the quiet of his apartment, calling out his son's mother's name. "I really miss our baby." Tears came to his eyes. "And I miss us." He sat for a long time in his chair in the quiet of his room.

After most of the images from all the years had subsided, and the unexpected tears dried, for no reason he could fathom, Wilbur remembered seeing a photograph somewhere recently of a gorilla named Julia at the Bronx Zoo. She was thirty-three years old but had, to the surprise of everyone, just given birth to a new baby. The keepers didn't know yet whether the baby was a boy or girl. The gorilla's father, named Ernie, was thirty one years old. It had been sixteen years since any baby gorillas has been born at the zoo. All assumed they were just too old. These gorillas were members of an endangered species.

Wilbur had been captivated by the new baby at that zoo. He had been particularly struck by the photograph of a large, clearly old and graying gorilla, tenderly holding her tiny, tiny little bundle. Both Julia, the old mama gorilla and the little baby, were gazing at the camera with brown eyes filled with wonder and love.

For a long while, Wilbur stared into space, chewing on his finger, trying to calculate just how far it might be to New York City and the Bronx Zoo. Twelve hundred miles, at least. Much further than he had been planning. But his old truck was still running clean, smooth. He could maybe do it in a couple of days. That'd be silly, though. Absolutely no reason to do something like that. He'd never been to New York City.

He bit his lower lip, thinking. Then went to the front door, picked up his suitcase, left the baby bags, went out and locked the door behind him.

A light rain was falling, four days later, as Wilbur stood in front of the cage, in the middle of the small crowd, all straining their necks to catch a glimpse of mama and baby.

22.

Replicable Studies

"This guy here says we have sixty-thousand thoughts a day," Holly said to Cork, looking up from her magazine. "And that fifty-nine thousand of them are the same thoughts we had the day before."

Holly was sitting on the tan living room couch in their small two bedroom home, reading her magazine. Cork was ten feet away, at the kitchen table, reassembling a fishing reel he had, over the past week, cleaned, oiled and restrung. He looked up, holding one of the last screws in place.

Corcoron Purvis—Cork—had been Facilities Maintenance Manager for Braxton Office Supplies for twenty-eight years, which is a fancy way of saying he had been head janitor at the squat, three story Braxton building for most of his adult life. The building was actually four stories if you counted the basement, where Cork's small office and large workshop were located.

Cork had no complaints. It was a decent job, sometimes challenging but mostly routine, a livable wage, regular hours, annual vacation, health insurance and all the normal holidays. He had companionable coworkers and a boss who trusted Cork's judgment and mostly left him alone, which was fine with Cork.

Cork's wife Holly was the Front Office Manager for A-1 Storage, which is a fancy way of saying she was the only secretary, receptionist and tenderer of the office coffee machine. She and Cork had been married for seventeen years—second marriage for both of them. A-1 didn't offer Holly the benefits or salary or companionable co-workers that Cork enjoyed—she mostly worked alone in a small almost shed-like office taking in rents and handling details of people moving in and out of their storage units, but it was an okay job and she had been there seven years.

"How does anybody know how many thoughts we have in a day?" Cork asked, incredulous.

"I guess they just count them," Holly said.

"You can't count somebody's thoughts all day long," Cork said.

"Maybe they just count them for an hour or two and then . . ."

"Not even an hour," Cork said. "You couldn't count your thoughts for an hour. Maybe a minute or two, at most."

"I don't know. That's just what he says," Holly said, looking back down at her magazine. "And he says the thoughts we have today are mostly the same we had yesterday."

"Okay let's try it," Cork said, returning to his fishing reel and quickly tightening the last screw into place. He set the reel down. "Let's count 'em."

"Count what?"

"Our thoughts," Cork said. He stood from the table and went into the kitchen, took the kitchen timer from the top of the microwave and went back into the living room. He dropped into his normal easy chair, across from Holly.

"Ready?" he asked.

"What?"

"We're going to count our thoughts for . . ." he looked at the timer, pushed buttons, ". . .two minutes."

"How do we count thoughts?" Holly asked.

"You just said he said we have sixty thousand thoughts a day. You believe everything you read in a magazine? Let's test it. Let's see."

Holly stared at Cork, her mouth half open. Then she laughed a half-laugh. "No thoughts are coming," she said.

"That's a thought right there," Cork said, grinning.

"Yes, I guess so," Holly said.

"Okay, ready?"

"I probably only have about four thoughts a minute," Holly said. "I'm really slow."

"There's two thoughts right there," Cork said. "Let's see. Let's count. Ready?"

"How? How will we count them?"

Cork thought about it. "We'll use our fingers," he said, holding up his hands and moving his thumb across his fingers. "So we don't lose track. We'll just do it for two minutes. Okay? Ready?"

"Well, okay," Holly said, grinning, setting down her magazine. "But this is dumb. You're going to see how dumb I am."

"No, it doesn't matter what the thoughts are. Just how many. We won't talk for two minutes. We'll just count thoughts. Ready?"

"I guess so."

"Okay, ready, set, go." A small beep as Cork pushed the timer.

They stared at each other, quiet, grinning, their fingers moving, counting. Two minutes later, the timer beeped.

"I lost count," Holly said.

"Me too. And I couldn't tell where one thought stopped and another thought started," Cork said.

"Yeah, me too," Holly said.

"But I counted about sixty," Cork said.

"Sixty? Wow," said Holly.

"But it's tricky," Cork said. "You don't realize you're having a thought until after it goes, and then it's like two thoughts when you're thinking about a thought going."

"What's the difference between a thought and a feeling?" Holly asked. "Or a seeing. Like I see you sitting there, is that a thought?"

"It's tricky," Cork said again. "What's a thought and what's not a thought. I don't know how that guy figures we have sixty thousand thoughts a day, or how they count thoughts."

They stared at each other.

"Let's try it again," Cork said.

"I wonder if they're counting dreams," Holly said. "Or if that's sixty thousand while you're awake."

"Good question. Let's see . . ." he reached over and grabbed a pencil off the side table and an envelope, and starting calculating. "If you sleep eight hours a night, that leaves sixteen hours. So that's . . .

Holly stared at him as he did the calculations.

"That's nine hundred and sixty minutes in a day," He said. "So if we have sixty thousand thoughts, that would mean. . ." he did more calculations. "Sixty-two point five. That's sixty two thoughts a minute. About one thought every second."

"I don't think that fast," Holly said.

"Depends on what you mean by thoughts," Cork said.

"If thoughts are feelings, then yeah, okay," Holly said. "You're always feeling something, one way or another."

"Or what you see. You don't have to think about it to know it's a lamp. But when you see a lamp, you sort of think about it, just for a second."

"Maybe that's what they mean," Holly said, "when they said you always think about the same stuff you thought about yesterday. That's because you're seeing the same stuff."

"Should we try it again?" Cork asked.

"Okay. This time I'll try not to lose count," Holly said.

"And every thought counts," Cork said, and they both laughed at his play on words. "I mean feelings and seeings, they count as thoughts."

"Okay," Holly said. "I'll have a lot more then."

"Okay," Cork said. He watched Holly. "Ready. Set. Go."

They stared wide eyed at each other and both started counting, like they'd never counted before.

23.

The Long Tail

"So here we are on Happy Street. We finally climbed our way off the Mean Streets."

Lana's words surprised him. Marcus turned in his lawn chair to stare at her, whose hair had gone gray and her body soft in the years she had been by his side. They had parked their lawn chairs under tall hackberry trees on the strip of grass between the wide sidewalk and Mountain Avenue. The walk was wide enough for two people to walk abreast and a third to walk past in the other direction. It was the annual Tour-de-Fat bicycle extravaganza, originally sponsored by the local brewer of Fat Tire beer and meant as a take-off of the Tour de France. Instead of speed and endurance, however, the contest was for the craziest costume while riding a bicycle, or the craziest bicycle, or tricycle, by individuals or groups.

Among both townspeople and local university students, Tour de Fat had evolved into the modern equivalent of the Ancient's Fool's Day. Local bankers dressed up like ballerinas, librarians dressed like dance-hall floozies; pirates and kings and fairies and space aliens mounted bicycles, tri-cycles, quadra-cycles, long, short, tall, impossible, painted and ribboned and flagged and flowered for the annual parade down Mountain Avenue and a loop of five miles of surrounding blocks to end back in Old Town for a beer fest and band concerts, jugglers and side shows. Thousands and thousands of participants, laughing, shouting, throwing candy to onlookers.

"You think?" Marcus asked, reaching for Lana's hand, staring into her eyes, letting the parade go by.

"We're in Disneyland," she said.

"Oh yeah," Marcus laughed. A bartender at a pub in Old Town had told them how the old-fashioned Main Street in the original Disneyland in Anaheim had been modeled after Fort Collins. "The guy came from here," the bartender assured them.

"Valley of the Jolly Green Giant," Marcus added.

"Ho, ho, ho," Laura smiled softly, squeezing his hand. Their real estate agent had driven them to the top of Bingham Hill on the western edge of Fort Collins to overlook a long, wide, green valley nestled against the foothills of the Rockies. "The artist who painted the original advertisements for the Jolly Green Giant grew up around here," the real estate agent bragged. Sure enough. Pleasant Valley, as it was known, resembled, sans elves, the advertisements.

Several small wrapped Tootsie Rolls landed at their feet. They looked back to the parade.

"For you young lovers," a young man on stilts called out. He wore face paint and a top hat. Along with bike riders, many costumed walkers were part of the parade. The young stilt man waved at them and walked awkwardly on, throwing candy. Marcus leaned down and picked up the Tootsie Rolls, handed one to Lana.

"Care for a hit?" the man in the lawn chair on the other side of Marcus asked, holding his breath, extending a joint.

"No thanks," Marcus said.

"Sure, I would," Lana said, reaching over Marcus to take the spiff.

"That's right, this is Colorado, land of the free," Marcus said, looking between the stranger and Lana. "It's legal. But I thought you were supposed to do this indoors, not in public."

"Tour de Fat, dude," the man said, letting out his toke. "Anything goes."

"It's been a long time," Lana said, as she took a large breath of pot.

A large hand landed on Lana's shoulders just as a short, crop-haired woman from the parade stopped in front of their chairs and snapped a picture.

"Got it," she said.

"Sorry ma'am, it's illegal to do that out here. We'll have to take you in, " a large policeman said, standing behind Lana with his hand on her shoulder.

"Wait a minute, wait a minute," Marcus said, standing up, knocking over his lawn chair to see the uniformed officer. "She just took . . ."

"Still not allowed in public," the officer gently interrupted.

"Hey, chill, it's Tour de Fat," the stranger who had offered her the joint argued from his chair.

"Still illegal in public," the officer repeated, and then grinned big. "Don't worry. It's no big deal. I was kidding about taking you in. It's a fifty dollar fine, max. Probably not even that. Probably won't even charge you. But we need to show a presence here. The law's the law. Can't let things get too out of hand, even on Tour de Fat, or especially on Tour de Fat. Figured I needed to tap some oldies, just to show I'm not being prejudiced. So just need to see some ID, let the boss know I'm out here working, not goofing off."

"No, no," Marcus said. "That's not fair. It wasn't hers. She didn't even . . ." Marcus turned to the stranger who had handed Lana the joint. He and his lawn chair had disappeared into the crowd.

That night, Marcus and Lana packed up their few belongings, loaded the Oldsmobile and headed for Montana. They knew when the misdemeanor citation hit the network, their aliases would be traced. There's no statute of limitations for charges of murder one, even in Disneyland.

24.

The Nelsons Move On

"Something's wrong with this house," Belinda said when she first walked in. "The vibes aren't right."

Bruce, who had been living in the house for three weeks, looked surprised and disappointed. When they had transferred from Chicago, Bruce had bought the house after looking at photos on line and after an independent inspector said the plumbing, heating, the roof and foundation all passed muster. It had seemed okay to him.

Over the next several weeks Belinda burned sage, lit candles and did cleansing rituals. Still, she was not at peace in the house.

"Oh sweetie, we're so glad to have a normal family move in," Gladys, two doors down, said one day over coffee. "The Nelsons fought all the time, knock down, drag out. He beat the kids, and beat her, too, I'm sure. The police were called numerous times. We were so glad to see them go, and your lovely family move in."

"Do you or anybody have photos of them?" Belinda asked.

"Of the Nelsons? Well, maybe. We had a neighborhood barbecue. The Nelsons came, acting sweet as pie."

Belinda called on neighbors over the next week and collected photos of the Nelsons. The neighbors worried that a different kind of kook had moved in. Belinda put the Nelson's photos on her bedroom altar and, along with other rituals, she prayed for peace in the Nelson's family.

Six months later Lucinda, six doors down and across the street, came to tea.

"What a peaceful home you have here," she said on entering. The next morning, Belinda put the photos of the Nelsons in a large box she labeled, "answered prayers."

25.

Omaha Meatloaf and Earmuffs

"So, are you going to Omaha or L.A.?"

Bridgette stared at Dominick, challenging. He returned her stare a long moment as he took in and let out a deep breath. He held his coffee cup with both hands, elbows on the table.

"I notice you didn't ask are we going to Omaha or L.A.," he finally said.

"I wasn't aware that this was a we decision," Bridget immediately shot back.

They had come to a tipping point, obviously, in this relationship. And had come to after-dinner coffee and a small shot of ouzo at Pucelli's small Italian restaurant on Denver's Colfax Avenue, a dozen blocks up the hill from the Capital. They each had apartments nearby, his on the north side of Colfax, hers on the more expensive south side. When the question arose, as it often did, "Your place or mine," the answer was most often hers, simply because it was warmer, roomier and in fact safer, the north side being a bit dicey at times. In the four years he'd needed to finish his dissertation he'd twice been robbed at gunpoint by desperate druggies.

"If this was a we decision," Dominick said, "Which would you choose? Or do I even need to ask?"

"Yea, right, duh," Bridgette said. She finally stopped staring at him, dropping her eyes to sip first her ouzo, then her coffee, holding her own cup in two hands.

Dominick let out a small laugh. "What? You'd rather be in warm, sunny, beautiful people L.A., ten minutes from the beach, California dreaming, than cold, gray, meatloaf and earmuffs Omaha?"

"Again, I didn't know this was a mutual decision," Bridgette said, lifting her eyes over the coffee cup to stare at him. They stared at each other. She dropped her eyes again. "And I'm not sure it should be. Or that I want it to be." She sipped her coffee, looked back up at him.

"This is your future, Dom," she said, "We obviously have something going here that's very nice, and tender and innocent."

"I don't know about innocent," Dominick laughed.

"Playful," Bridgette said. "Innocent of implications, demands."

"Like monogamy," Dominick said, not playful. "No demands for monogamy."

Bridgette set her coffee cup down, avoiding his eyes, and again picked up her ouzo and sipped.

"Sorry," Dominick said. "Didn't mean to be crude."

Now Bridgette moved the ouzo glass to the end of her fingertips on both hands. "Not crude," she said. "Just clumsy."

"Sorry," Dominick said softly.

They had grown closer and closer over the previous eighteen months, spending most weekends together and many week nights. Dominick had finally turned in his revised thesis, titled, *Levels of Variability in Peripheral Arterial Diseases*. He was preparing for his oral defense. He had already been offered a post-doctorate position at the Omaha Center of Biomedical Research Excellence to help in their study of "movement affecting disorders." He had also applied for, and been accepted at Antioch College, in Los Angeles, mostly teaching introductory biomechanical principles.

Bridgette was a senior financial advisor for Wells Fargo. Although Dominick had been too busy and focused on his own research to have more than one relationship, he knew he was only one of three men in Bridgette's life, though it seemed, at least to him, he was the leading man. Early in their relationship there had been many weekend nights when Bridgette was "busy," already committed elsewhere. These nights still occasionally happened, though not as often. She was mostly available when Dominick had time, but not always.

"So, Wells Fargo has branches in both Omaha and L.A., and if you wanted to . . ." Dominick said, dropping the subject of monogamy.

"Dominick, you decide where you want to go," Bridgette said. "It's your future. Your life. It's a very important choice. And then after you decide, we can decide about our future, our life."

"I really love you, Bridge. Really want to be with you. Want you to be part of my future."

"Oh Dom," she said, putting her ouzo down and reaching across and putting her hand on his. "You know I feel the same way. We really do have something special. But this is... this is bigger than us."

Dominick put his other hand on hers. "I have the feeling," he said, "If I chose L.A., you'd be more likely to go, more likely to ask for a transfer than if I chose Omaha."

She looked at him a long moment. "Yes, you're probably right," she said. "Have you been to Omaha?"

Dominick laughed, looking at her, and not for the first time sensing her deep strength, her natural independence, her probable future without him, regardless of whether he chose Omaha or the City of Angels. Even though it didn't move, he could feel her hand slipping away.

26.

Leaving the Lion's Lair

"Please, Louise, give me a moment to think. "

"You don't need to think, Leonard," Louise whispered without missing a beat. "You don't need to be somebody special, somebody far away. Just be who you are, right here. Right now. You don't need to think to be who you already are."

Leonard looked through the bars to Louise and curiously, mysteriously, wondrously, in that moment no more thoughts came. For a short while, they both just breathed, perhaps even in unison, and Leonard had no thoughts. Louise smiled.

"There now," she said, her eyes twinkling, as if she'd just told the punch line of a good joke, catching him, again, holding him, as she had time after time since sixth grade.

"Now, don't think," she continued. "Do you still love me? Do you want to be with me again?"

"But that isn't what you asked..." Leonard started to say.

"Don't think. Just answer. Do you love me?"

"Of course I do. You know I do. But..."

"Then what's there to think about?"

Again, Leonard's thoughts stopped. And then slowly, clearly, a single thought came, like a jet plane trailing a white contrail across a clear blue sky: if any woman could look beautiful wearing lime green county jail fatigues, without makeup, her hair cut short, at least thirty pounds too many on her almost six foot frame, if any woman could look beautiful, that woman was Louise. Leonard knew from long experience it wasn't just her outer features that made her beautiful. It was her lioness presence, shining through those eyes, as if she wanted to eat you like a rabbit because you looked so yummy. Those eyes stopped thoughts.

"Okay," he said softly.

His okay brought up her smile. And then he thought, again quite clearly, it was these eyes, and this smile, the eyes and smile right here, that brought him three hundred and fifty miles to the visiting room of her county jail, two days before she was scheduled to be transferred to Canon City, the Colorado State Penitentiary, six to nine years for armed robbery, third offense, the judge being lenient even with that. Men, even District judges, were always lenient when Louise was involved.

"Okay, time's up," the officer said, coming back into the room.

Leonard and Louise said nothing more, just watched each other a brief moment. It had been over three years since he had last seen her, on her way to Texas, with that new boyfriend. Louise nodded at him, smiling, her eyes questioning, *yes?* Leonard silently nodded back, *yes.*

As he was led back through the metal doors of the county correctional unit Leonard's mind was numb, as if in a daze at the daring magnitude of what Louise had just asked.

"Stay warm out there," the officer said as he held open the final metal door that led into the lobby. Leonard nodded his head. The metal door shut behind him. He pulled the brown stocking cap from the pocket of his old leather jacket and fitted it firmly on his head, pulling it over his ears. He wrapped his wool scarf around his neck and zipped the jacket up tight. He walked outside into the cold, blowing January snow.

Walking across the crowded parking lot toward his car, hands in pockets, hunched against the wind, Leonard started to think about what had just happened, what he had agreed to do. Even before he reached his old truck his thoughts started tumbling faster and faster and faster and faster and faster, like boulders tumbling down a mountain. He couldn't get out of their way. His face contracted in a grimace, his thoughts hurt him so much.

Bahama Will-Power

"You could just get a regular job, something simple this time, like everybody else," Maureen said, leaning back on her beach chair, her dark sunglasses shielding her from the bright Bermuda sun. Her drinks and magazine were on the small aluminum folding table beside her chair. Her tan was almost perfect now—except for the white under her bikini, of course. Robert often said he preferred a full, round woman. He thought the white parts were sexy.

Robert was sitting on the sand, next to his own chair a few feet from Maureen, casually digging in the sand with a piece of driftwood.

"Wouldn't need to be full time or anything. Just something to keep you busy, keep your mind off things."

"Yeah, and then when I die, you could put that on my gravestone: *He kept his mind off things.*"

"Oh Robert," she said, reaching down and picking up her *People* magazine again. "Why are you always so hard on yourself?" She started flipping through the pages.

Robert stood up. "I guess I'll go for another walk," he said, throwing his piece of driftwood towards the outgoing tide. "You want to go?"

"No thanks," she said, her eye caught by an article about a Hollywood actress cheating on her Rap Star husband. "I'm good. Take your time."

As Robert walked down the beach he idly considered what a wake-up call it would be for Maureen if he just walked into the surf, started swimming toward the horizon, and then kept swimming and swimming and swimming until he could swim no more, too far away to ever swim back.

He stopped and stared at the horizon. The gulls squealed. Children and young lovers played in the shallows. The pulsing, rolling thunder of the crashing waves opened—or almost opened— some deep door inside.

At sixty-six, Robert was not especially fit, carrying an extra fifteen or twenty pounds. Okay, twenty-five. Exercise bored him to death. Still, he felt fairly healthy. He wondered how long he'd have to swim, straight out, before he reached the point of no-return. Not that long. Twenty minutes? Thirty minutes? Probably less than that.

Such a swim would be a fairly simple, direct, uncomplicated route to oblivion. Yes, the last five minutes might be bad— even panicky. Yet compared to all the other long, dreary, dreadful and possibly painful ways one might die—such as happened to both his mother and father for example—a mere five minutes of panic after a thirty minute swim seemed almost graceful.

Financially, Maureen would be okay. Their home in Peoria was mortgage free. A large chain had bought the copy center and mailing service business he'd built up over twenty-eight years. They'd made him an offer he couldn't refuse. The proceeds were now invested in safe annuities, blue chip stocks and bonds. His life insurance was paid up. It would look like an accident, double indemnity.

This was their third trip to the Bahamas in the last eighteen months. They liked it here. And it was a lot easier than those trips they'd taken in earlier years to Holland and Spain and Portugal. He'd liked Paris, but like Hawaii, it was so expensive and so crowded he couldn't relax. In the last seven years, with all those trips, both he and Maureen had pretty much squashed whatever travel bug they'd felt.

Robert continued to stare at the far horizon. He knew what he would need would be will-power. To just keep swimming, and not turn back, he'd have to fight his own mind, his own inner arguments, and his own biological urge toward survival. In order to do that, he assumed, he'd have to concentrate his will on the swimming itself. He'd have to fight through—swim through—all the mental, emotional and biological arguments that would surely rise to encourage him to turn back. A man would have to be very strong-willed, he saw, to fight through his own deep conditioning, not turn back, keep swimming. He wondered if he had the will-power in him to do that.

"Pardon me sir," a young lady's voice interrupted his thinking, his concentration on the far horizon. Robert turned to see a young, slightly overweight, somewhat frazzled-looking American woman, mid-twenties at most, with a badly fitting swimsuit standing next to him. She had tears in her eyes, as if she had been crying or was about to cry.

"I hate to ask you this, but my boyfriend made me." She looked along the far beach, and Robert's eyes followed to a skinny young man in bathing suit walking near the beach road.

"Yes?" Robert asked.

"We're in a really tight spot. For a hundred dollars, would you like to sleep with me?"

Suddenly, the spell was broken. Robert spontaneously laughed. It was a deep laugh, more natural, more healthy, more genuine than any laugh he had laughed in years. The young lady's tears started falling.

"I told him I was not worth . . ."

"Of course, sweetie, I would love to sleep with you," Robert interrupted. "And a hundred dollars is way, way too little for what you're worth."

"Really?" the young girl asked, eyes wide, no longer crying. "I haven't done this. . ."

Robert stepped over and put his arm around her, in a fatherly way. "Oh love," he said. "You're worth at least a million. But before we can discover your true worth, we need to untangle you from the clutches of the scuzz ball who would ask you to do such a thing."

"No, no, he's really not that . . ." The young woman started to argue.

"Yes he is, just watch," Robert interrupted.

Robert knew his will power was strong enough to get this little job done.

"And as far as sleeping with you, no need. I'm already well taken care of in that department."

Suddenly, Robert was very glad to be alive, right here, right now. He beamed at the young woman.

28.

The Ruins

Sitting inside the cab of his Cat 345 DL excavator, Johnny Phipps was surprised to feel a certain secret relief in this latest project--tearing down old St. Bartholomew's – Saint Bart's, as the old folks used to call it when he was a kid going to church here. Saint Fart's as he and his buddies named it.

After years of bitter wrangling, legal challenges involving the Historical Preservation Committee and the Downtown Development Authority and state and even federal interests, the developers for a new Best Buy had finally won. Renovations to the church, first built "on this site" (which eventually were the damning operative words) in 1683, had been continuous and extensive and not always—or even often—in keeping with or in respect for its original structure. Its latest owners—or at least users—were a theater group who had been unable to keep up payments and the title had reverted again to First National Bank. St Bart's itself had moved in 1983, when

Johnny Phipps was thirteen, to a newer, larger brick, steel and glass edifice on the edge of the southern suburbs. His folks continued to attend the suburban church for a number of years—indeed, they had contributed part of their tithe to the new church building fund. After years of Sunday morning battles, when Johnny's older sister, Shelly, turned sixteen she simply refused to go any more. "I'm old enough to know what I believe and what I don't," she said. Curiously, years later, after she was married with two kids, she returned to the church.

Shelly's refusal to attend church paved the way for Johnny himself to stop going a few months later. "If she doesn't have to, why do I?"

His folks switched to the Unitarian Church a few years later. At their urging, both he and Shelly checked it out several times on different Sundays, but it didn't take. A short while later, his folks then switched to Unity. One Sunday, driving home from church, his father had a heart-attack, crashed the Oldsmobile into a park bench, fortunately empty at the time, and died three days later. Johnny's mother, unhurt in the incident, never returned to either Unity or the Unitarian Church. The pastor from St. Bart's performed the funeral service, in the chapel of Goodrich Funeral home. Three years later, after a period of anger at God for His inattentiveness, and then at herself for lapsing, she returned to Saint Bart's in the burbs and has been a faithful servant ever since, particularly on the flower committee.

The old downtown Saint Bart's had been picked clean of relics, windows, doors, doorknobs, much of the molding and every usable, salable, salvageable item. Johnny and his Cat excavator, and the rest of the team working for Duncan Construction had been tearing it down now for two days, beginning with the roof, and then the walls, loading debris into trucks to haul to the landfill. They were now down to the foundation. Of course, Johnny himself didn't own the huge machine. It belonged to Duncan Construction, where he had worked the last nine years. They'd been really good to him, even helped pay for his schooling in Heavy Equipment Operation and to get his Commercial Driver's License.

Tearing down the roof and walls of old Saint Bart's had at first been somewhat sad for Johnny. Actually, the thought of it made him sad. Moving the large excavator into position to reach up with its large claw bucket had brought on melancholy, remembering his first years here, and his first communion, the simple child faith he had in what his elders were teaching. He knew, back then, that Jesus

135

really did love all the little children of the world, and he had been grateful for that.

The work also made him remember, and be both grateful for and melancholy about, his childhood family and the years growing up. Two days ago, after moving the machine into place, sitting next to the church inside the Cat's cab, feeling very grown up, a bit paunchy, but muscular, with a hard hat, he was very surprised when his heart suddenly melted in his chest and brought tears to his eyes. He was certain no one had noticed, but still . . .

Curiously, as he took the first bite out of the center roof, exposing what had once been the sanctuary to the open sky, it felt as if a window in the back of his head had opened—a window he hadn't known was there—and a cool breeze started to blow. As the splintered structure of old Saint Bart's was loaded into the beds of waiting trucks, Johnny felt a secret, long-standing weight likewise lifting. As he worked, methodically moving bucketful after bucketful into the trucks, he noticed that the sadness and melancholy turned to a secret joy, even serenity, rising up in him.

Now, today, they were working on removing the foundation. He pulled the levers and pushed the pedals to almost gently slide the bucket underneath one of the oldest of stones from the original church. A local landscape design company had contracted to purchase these stones. Their flatbed truck was parked and idling nearby, waiting to haul the chest-high stones to their new location. Johnny had already loaded half a dozen of them onto the truck and had turned his machine to upload the next stone. The driver and two of the landscape crew were watching. Johnny lifted the stone.

Suddenly, both men started waving their arms, shouting, "Wait! Wait! Stop! Stop!" Johnny had the stone in the air, and knew he needed to move it to safety. In spite of their shouts, He smoothly swung it away from the foundation and lifted it onto the waiting flatbed. The two men had climbed down into the hole. They were excitedly pointing, calling to others to come. Johnny shut off the engine and climbed out of the cab.

When he got down into the hole with them, he could see what they saw. It was a human skull, cocked sideways, severed from the top of a skeleton half covered by the next stone. He could see a few remnants of old clothing. The skull, and skeleton had been under the large stone he had just moved to the flatbed.

"Woe, dude," the young guy from the landscape design company said as

Johnny approached. One hand of the skeleton clutched a rusted, broken cross over what would have been his heart.

29.

Existential Whispers

"Good night boys. Thanks. Had a great time giving you my money."

Griggs, his back turned to the guys, waved his hand over his head, slipped out the door into the cool of the night.

"Come again when you have more dough," one of the guys shouted after him, and the other guys laughed. Griggs smiled, and let the comment go. He was already too far down the walk to shout back, "up yours," as the guys would expect.

Griggs actually hadn't lost that much money. A few bucks, at most. Nobody ever lost much money. Betting nickels, dimes and quarters, fifty cents maximum, they played as if it were fivers, tens and fifties.

They'd been playing poker, once a month or so, for over fifteen years, mostly in the kitchen of Jeb Stuart's old ramshackle duplex, since he was the only bachelor.

Griggs was one of the four regular players, with semi-regulars filled in with either friends from work or neighbors or best friends of friends. After fifteen years of such meet-ups, spending three or four hours drinking beer, sometimes puffing a little weed, playing all variations of poker, there were no strangers among them.

Although they drank, nobody usually got drunk at these games, and those who did so were generally not asked back. But Griggs would get a buzz on, like he had right now. Griggs and his wife Joan lived less than a dozen blocks from Jeb, so Griggs would normally walk, especially on a brisk spring night like this. No reason to chance a DUI. As a lawyer, he knew: driving buzzed was driving drunk.

"You're quite the social butterfly," Joan had teased him tonight as he left for poker. "Last night book club. Monday night board meeting for the hiking club, church picnic on Sunday . . ."

"Just a popular guy," Griggs had said.

Walking home alone, now, in the late night cool air, the sound of crickets nearby and the traffic in the distance, Griggs was disappointed to realize that, once again, and still, he felt vaguely trapped inside his skin. He stopped in the middle of the walk, under a hackberry tree, and unthinkingly let out a deep sigh.

He'd had high hopes for the poker game. He had told himself that poker was real guy stuff, with real guy talk, real guy laughs, where he could feel totally at home, totally at ease. And it was true. He and the guys did laugh and swear and tell dirty jokes and feel at home, at ease. And yet, even four hours playing poker with the guys didn't quite do it, didn't quite lift Griggs' growing sense of loneliness.

It'd been coming on him for months. Or perhaps, as he thought now, close to midnight and standing alone on the walk, the loneliness had always been there and only in the past several months had he become aware of it.

His marriage to Joan was great, as comfortable as an old pair of shoes. They could and did talk to each other about almost anything, though he didn't talk to her about this growing sense of loneliness. He felt she might take it personally, something lacking in her, in their marriage.

His hiking club was also great. He'd spend hours hiking in the woods with bright, upbeat companions, with continually changing scenery, different trails, different people. Yet even here, they'd go up, come down, leave him with himself.

His book club was the same way. Great books, lots of laughs, stimulating conversation and then he'd be alone again, with himself, inside his skin again. The people at church were likewise bright and cheery. The church was mostly Joan's thing. Nothing against them. He knew he'd have fun at the upcoming picnic, have a chance to talk with people he admired, got along with. But there was a depth in him that his hiking or the church picnic, or book club or poker was not reaching. He was feeling a growing sense of loneliness that human companionship apparently could not lift.

"Everything okay, Griggs?" Bascom Stoltz called out from the front walk. Bascom had also left the game and was heading toward his car. Bascom's shout surprised him. Griggs hadn't realized he'd been stopped so long on the walk, or so close.

"Yeah, yeah," Griggs called, walking forward again, raising his hand again. "Everything fine. Just trying to figure out which way home."

Winter's Coming

"Dad, really, don't you think it's time to give up the house? Go to a retirement community?"

Lemont glared at his daughter. She stopped talking. He was sitting on the hospital bed with his legs hanging over the edge. His feet didn't touch the floor.

"Now don't give me that look," his daughter started again. "You're just being a stubborn old goat."

"I need my pants and my shirt," Lemont said. He had a three day stubble of white beard coming through his deeply wrinkled and sun baked face. The silly one-size-fits-all hospital gown was three sizes too big.

"They still need to examine you. You can't get dressed yet."

"In that closet, right there." Lemont pointed to the closet next to the bathroom.

"No, dad, it's not time yet."

Lemont started to move his hips forward. He flinched with pain and stopped.

"There, you see. You're not anywhere near ready to go."

Lemont moved again, and flinched in pain again, but this time kept moving and gingerly, carefully lowered himself off the bed.

"Da--ad" his daughter complained. "Okay, okay, " she said, standing from the beside chair. "Stay there. I'll get them. Just don't move." She went across the room, opened the closet, took out a woolen shirt and khaki pants, both still on hangers.

"I have an undershirt there somewhere," Lamont said.

His daughter looked, saw nothing, turned back. "Maybe in the drawer there beside you," she said.

"You look, please," Lemont said, still standing next to the bed. His daughter went to the nightstand.

"So okay, keep the house," she said. "It doesn't have to be permanent. But right now, you need to go somewhere, be somewhere you can recuperate. The doctor said Medicare would pay . . ."

"Is my undershirt in there?" Lemont asked. His daughter was looking in the bedside drawer.

"No, it's not," she said, laying the shirt and pants still in their hangers on the unmade bed.

"It's here somewhere. I came in with it."

His daughter walked back across the room and disappeared into the closet. "Here it is," she said from inside the closet. "On the shelf. I didn't see it."

The door opened and a young female doctor wearing hospital greens entered, followed by a nurse wearing similar garb. The doctor had a stethoscope around her neck.

"Well, well, well," she said, "Look who's up and about."

"I told him he shouldn't," the daughter said, coming out of the closet.

"You feeling better?" the doctor asked.

"Good enough to go home," Lemont said. "I'm going home. Laura Lee, bring me my shirt."

"Now dad, listen to what the doctor has to say," his daughter pleaded.

"I'll walk out of here wearing this butt-window dress if I have to," Lemont said. "But one way or another, I'm leaving."

"Da--ad," Laura Lee said.

"I'm going," Lemont said. "In the next five minutes. You going to bring me that shirt or not?"

"I'll have to fill out a form and have you sign it," the doctor said. "That you're leaving against medical advice."

"Well then, get the damn form, because I'm leaving on my own advice," Lemont said.

It wasn't five minutes, but thirty-five minutes later Lemont, fully dressed, was wheeled out the front door of Standbridge Medical Center, following the rigid rule that every patient must use the wheel chair provided to exit the facility.

Once outside, Lemont slowly, painfully stood up, holding onto Laura Lee's forearms. Once up he took a deep breath and stared up at the October sky. "Okay," he said, still holding her arm. "Let's go."

"Why don't I just go get the car," she said.

"Let's go," he said again. And slowly, together, they headed toward the nearby parking lot.

"I'll call tomorrow," Laura Lee said when she had him ensconced again on his couch. The old living room was cluttered, the small home at the edge of town now musty. Laura Lee had grown up in this house. "Unless you want me to stay."

"Nope, like I said, I'll be fine. Just fine. Thank you for all you have done."

When he heard her car door slam, the engine start and her car finally pulling out of the drive, he settled back into the couch, let out a deep breath, closed his eyes. Here on his own couch, in his own room, alone, with the familiar light, he could finally relax, start to mend again.

The next morning when Laura Lee called, Lemont was outside, at the wood pile, slowly, gingerly chopping more wood. He sensed it could be a long, hard winter. He wanted to be ready.

A Million Good Guys

"Why do movies always have bad people in them?"

Morey Bernstein wasn't old enough yet to be sitting in the front seat, so his question came floating up from the back. Maureen looked into the rear view mirror to study her little guy.

"Was it a scary movie, honey?"

"Not really. I was just wondering."

Maureen turned her eyes back to the road. And then, after a long pause, she said, "That's a good question. I guess they want to make it more exciting. Maybe we should ask grandpa."

Harriet Lansing had picked up the other three boys after the Saturday matinee, but Maureen's father, Bennie, had just come home from the hospital the previous Thursday and now they were all having an early dinner together to celebrate his recovery.

"Was this movie as good as the last one?" Maureen asked, again checking Morey in the rear view mirror.

"Yeah, I guess. Maybe not. Yeah probably," Morey said, obviously not sure how he felt about Space Invaders 4: Revenge of the Trojans.

Morey was grateful to be simply watching the ordinary street scenes pass outside. Buildings that were not tumbling down in flames. Windows that were not breaking. People walking on the sidewalk, or waiting on benches for the bus. The people outside the car window were not being blasted away or flying around or running for their lives. He liked the gray clouds and the people in their coats. He hoped it would snow, so the world would go even slower.

"Okay, here we are," Maureen said, ten minutes later, pulling to the curb in front of a small frame house, with neatly trimmed bushes tucked between two larger, more modern but less well-kept homes. "Be sure to give your grandpa a big hug. He's missed you. And hasn't been feeling good."

"I know," Morey said, unbuckling his seat belt. He waited for his mother to come around and open his door.

"Hey there, young sir," Grandpa Bennie said, opening the glass screen door as Maureen and Morey walked onto the porch. He had obviously been waiting and watching for them.

"Hey dad, should you be up?" Maureen asked.

"Hi grandpa," Morey said.

"Sure. I'm fine. I'm fine. Come in, come in," Grandpa Bennie said, holding the screen door wide.

As Morey went by, his grandpa patted him on the head and Morey briefly patted him on the hip. Maureen kissed her dad on the cheek.

"Good to see you up and about," she said.

"Yeah, yeah, your mother has been taking good care of me. I'm fine."

When they were in the house, door closed, taking off their coats, giving them to Grandpa Bennie, he asked, "So how was the movie?"

"Pretty good," Morey said.

"As good as the other ones?" Bennie asked.

"No, not really," Morey said, apparently having decided.

"Oh that's too bad," Grandpa Bennie said, hanging up the coats.

"Hey look who's here," Grandma Louise said, coming out of the kitchen drying her hands on a dish towel.

After dinner, when the ladies were in the kitchen doing dishes, Morey put down the old I-Pad they kept for him and looked at his grandpa who was reading the newspaper.

"Grandpa, why are there always bad people in the movies?"

Grandpa Bennie looked up from the newspaper. He looked at Morey for a long while, nodding his head slightly, thinking about it. They watched each other.

"Because movies are make-believe," he finally said.

"Are there bad guys in real life?"

Again, Grandpa Bennie nodded his head, thinking about it a long while. "There's mostly good guys," he said. "Not like the movies. In the movies it's one to one or even five bad guys to one of the good guys. In real life, it's a hundred good guys, or even a thousand good guys, maybe ten thousand good guys, to every bad guy."

Morey studied him and thought about this. "Might there be maybe even a million good guys to one bad guy? Morey asked.

"Yes, yes, I think you're right. A million good guys, in real life, to every bad guy. A million to one, at least, in real life."

"That's good," Morey said, nodding his head in agreement, looking at his Grandpa. "I like that much better. Real life makes more sense."

Morey looked back at his I-pad, and Grandpa Bennie grinned at him.

Acknowledgements

Some of these stories have appeared in print and/or online. For permission to reprint, the author wishes to thank,

A Flash in the Pan, for *Morphic Resonance;* **Splickety Publications**, for *Understandably Not Talkative;* **The Iconoclast,** for *Probably a Family Man;* **Saturday Night Reader**, for *The Good Life* and **Ink Sweat and Tears** for *A Million Good Guys.*

I'd also like to thank Michael Bailey, David Bye, John Gascoyne and Robert Orr for their helpful editing, proof-reading and Lexus-level friendship.

Bear Jack Gebhardt

bear@heartmountainmonastery.com

606 Hanna St.
Fort Collins, CO. 80521

May peace and joy and a consistent, spunky clarity be yours every day on your pilgrimage ...

--- *Bear G.*

Christmas, 2015